COTSWOLD CRIME AND CORRUPTION

Cotswold Crime and Corruption

Unearthing Victorian Secrets

Gail Fulton

YOUCAXTON
PUBLICATIONS

ISBN 978-1-913425-79-1
Published by YouCaxton Publications 2021
YCBN: 01

YouCaxton Publications
www.youcaxton.co.uk

Dedication

To my wonderful late parents, especially my dearest father, who once recounted visiting his friend in a Dr. Barnado's home when he was very young. As a child myself, his story deeply touched me and it has surfaced decades later, as inspiration for this book. He taught me the joy of writing and was always there with patient encouragement, endless loving support and belief in my endeavours. I love and miss you both dearly.

Acknowledgements

My thanks to my darling husband Rob, who patiently proof read my efforts, checked out my random thoughts on Google and made copious cups of tea whilst tolerating my tapping away for hours at a time.

To our two beautiful daughters, Nikki and Becky and future son-in-law Chris, who show me constant love and support, for which I am truly grateful. Thank you for your encouragement and interest. I love you always and forever.

Not least, a huge offering of thanks to my dearest friends Susie and Pete M., who kindly agreed to read my first very rough script and who subsequently gave me the courage to have this put to print. You're the best!!

Further appreciation to Annie J. for her sound advice and guidance on publication.

§

Contents

Chapter 1 1

Chapter 2 10

Chapter 3 14

Chapter 4 25

Chapter 5 32

Chapter 6 35

Chapter 7 48

Chapter 8 53

Chapter 9 57

Chapter 10...63

Chapter 11...69

Chapter 12...74

Chapter 13...78

Chapter 14...83

Chapter 15...90

Chapter 16..101

Chapter 17..108

Chapter 18..114

Chapter 19..118

Chapter 20..126

Chapter 21..136

Chapter 22..150

Chapter 23..158

Chapter 24..168

Chapter 25..174

Chapter 26..185

Chapter 27..191

Chapter 28..198

Chapter 29..211

About the Author 212

Chapter 1

AUTUMN 1862

Louise's thoughts seemed compelled to re-visit the side of a grave. Tears welled uncontrollably as though she sat there still, mourning her loss. The familiar, raw pain in her chest grew unbidden and she stifled a sob, jolting her back to the present. Blinking hard against heavy tears, she realized it had been some time since she had allowed herself to remember in this way. The mind's protective filter had momentarily collapsed and permitted the ever present but suppressed grief to hurt again.

Sitting now at her dressing table looking absentmindedly through her window towards the fields, mesmerised by the autumnal scene. The weather had, for weeks, been glorious and the leaves were now beginning to turn a blazing array of colour, in the warm late summer sunshine. She gave an involuntary heavy sigh, as her mind scrambled through a labyrinth of bitter-sweet memories. Despite the warmth of the sunshine settling on the rug beneath her stocking-less feet, a shiver passed over her, as she contemplated the weight of sadness, which hung around her like a heavy black curtain.

She instinctively closed her eyes, determined to focus on images of yesteryear, exploring in an instant, the immediate happiness of infant carefree days. Each memory linked by association through her mental filing cabinet of thought. In her mind's eye, Louise found herself and her sister walking back home along the dry path of the riverside as the early evening sun dipped into a pink and turquoise sky. Such vibrancy. Such joy. Without effort, she imagined herself once again in that protected and secure embrace of life.

Her thoughts continued to ramble. Summertime! Such an evocative word! Such reminiscence. She paused, as though emotionally saturated. It aroused a rush of childhood memories. An instant collage of pictorial images pushed through her subconscious mind and married with memories of smells – roses, fresh hay, lavender. She mentally summoned up the sound of the distant buzz of chatter from the field workers in the near distance. The sense of the sun's warmth on her skin. A cacophony of birdsong. Piglets squealing whilst their mother snorted among the muddy trough of food. She imagined lying in the meadow, daisy chains around their necks, laughing in the company of her dear sister, looking upwards to the endless blue summer sky and seeing shapes in the puffy wisps of clouds – a bear, a duck, a face... She could still feel the freshly cut corn stubble prickling into her back through the picnic rug and the tiny black corn midges annoying her skin – but it didn't matter. Another pie! Flick away a pesky wasp. Clatter of giggles and screeches.

Louise, could only see beauty in mother nature's artistic palette. She especially reveled in the colourful vibrancy yet homely comfort of autumn. The cosiness of cottages set amid autumnal morning foggy haze and that distinctive, woody smoke aroma belching from chimneys as early morning frost lay on the sparkling ground. The shorter days and longer evenings, brought Louise domestic images of warm milk and crunchy biscuit treats... and fun as she watched her breath visibly exit her mouth as she ran playing in the golden fields. Precious, rose coloured childhood retrospection. Yet, as the seasons crawled towards autumn, her dear mamma would dip into deep melancholy. Autumn, just like sunsets, provoked black moods in mamma. It evoked for her, the passing of another day of her life. Gone. Disturbing negativity. The dimness of light in the evenings would unsettle her and her sadness would become overwhelming.

Her gloom could be infectious, discomforting those who loved her. Louise felt a traitor, guilty for finding joy at the same time.

It was early October 1862. The symbolic drawing to a close of the calendar year was again looming and with it a firm reminder of the pain of the demise of maternal love and security. Louise still desperately missed her dear mamma. It was two years on, yet Louise still often found herself, fleetingly, back in that moment. Staring blankly, she had again found herself revisiting those random memories as her mind involuntarily selected scenarios from the depths of her subconscious, without any instruction from herself... It was as though someone else was inside her head, reminding her of a kaleidoscope of images, some of which she had revisited often since her mother's death. Others, she had not considered for a long time. Each thought, each memory, she would pick at until it was completely unraveled and the pain of that recollection peaked. Every moment of that shock and sadness engrained in her mind, would never be erased.

Her mother's premature departure broke Louise's heart. She had sat by her bedside for day after day, praying for a miracle to restore her to full health. It was so unfair! There was so much yet to learn from her. So many stories to share and memories yet to make. So much laughter yet to be had! They had always shared a close mother-daughter relationship and it had been said that Louise, as the much younger of the two daughters, had been unexpected and overly cherished.

To watch her mother slide away from her was punishing in

itself but to simultaneously watch her dearest papa grieving for the impending loss of his wife and loving soul mate, was just about too much to bear. It pained her so deeply. Such sadness was not only emotionally traumatic but gruelingly physical and without appetite, she herself began to lose weight. Ironically, the very person to cajole her from this downward spiral, would have been her dear mother. Without her, she was without direction or reason.

Downstairs and under the careful instruction of her father, Lord Thomas Dorchester, a large dusty, leather trunk had been lifted down from the attic, by two of the servants. Lord Dorchester had suddenly remembered the documents he had been searching for, were indeed likely to be found in here, where he suspected they had been secreted by his own parents, decades ago, for safe keeping. The men were sweating profusely under such duress of its heavy weight and simultaneously grunted as it was lowered to the floor in their master's drawing room. Dusting it off and struggling with the precious key to turn the now rusted lock, finally the lid was satisfyingly opened.

Astonished to find such an unexpected cache of ribbon bound papers, Lord Dorchester proceeded to spend his entire morning totally absorbed in leafing through the treasure trove of history. Ultimately finding what he needed, he put the preserved document to one side with relief. It was time now, he believed, to get his affairs in order so that, should anything happen to him, his two daughters would be able to inherit his estate without stress or obstacle. He would leave such documentation with his solicitor for that purpose.

Re-organising then the papers within the trunk, his eyes fell upon an unfamiliar assemblage of parchment. Readjusting his pince-nez, he squinted at the finely written script. In disbelief, he read it again. Taking it towards the daylight to be sure he was reading correctly, his heart bruised at its contents and he slowly shook his head in something close to horror. In shock, he gripped the edge of a chair for stability and slowly sank into it, without taking his eyes off the words in front of him. It would appear, (he paused and flicked the pages again), that this document did indeed refer to ... his own dear mother! He stared again in disbelief. My God!! He never knew this!!...

Autumn, no matter how Mother Nature dressed the season, became a mentally tortuous reminder of Louise's bereavement. She thought of her sister and mused about her life. Elspeth was utterly besotted with her good fortune: She had met a dashingly handsome soldier and they had made a wonderful life for themselves in London and had welcomed not one but two gorgeous children. The twins had become her life and whilst they still kept in touch as sisters, their lives had diverted so much, that they seemed to have little in common. Apart from a monthly exchange of letters, they knew little of each other's lives. She was pleased for Elspeth. She deserved all her happiness but she missed her too and felt she had lost her big sister forever and that further enhanced her sadness and sense of loss.

Watching his daughter's change in demeanour and seeing a pattern being repeated at this time of year, Lord Dorchester, observed her with concern. Unlike many men of his generation, he was unfashionably able to sit in quiet companionship with his daughter and talk to her with ease. They shared many topics of interest in life and their bond was unusually close – one might even say, spiritual. They themselves recognised their own blessing in having each other and it was this complete ease of relationship, which had brought them through the worst of the tough times. Without each other, they doubted either would have been able to brave out and survive what would otherwise have been intolerable times. Lord Dorchester noted his daughter's increasingly shadowy eyes in the morning, the less vibrancy in her voice and the passing comment others might miss when she remarked upon 'the autumnal light dying into winter'. He knew she wasn't just referring to the daylight but to a deeper light within herself.

With his usual kindly, warm thoughtfulness, he suggested one morning at breakfast that she should set off in advance of him to their country retreat, where he would of course join her for the Christmas season, as they always did. He had some of his own work to do and teasingly claimed a 'bit of peace and quiet' would do just the job!

Louise loved their country home with a passion. Set deep in the heart of the Cotswolds, the honey stoned façade of her childhood holiday residence, held a wealth of cherished recollections. Closing her eyes to envisage this haven, she invited images of happy family times into her mind. Each reminiscence was drenched in love. Walking through its welcoming doors was like wrapping a comfort blanket around her soul. This total act of selflessness of her father was no surprise to Louise for she knew he would miss her company and she realized without comment that he had recognized her downturn in mental stability. She could not hide anything from him – nor would she really wish to. However, equally, she would value some time – just a few weeks - to be entirely herself and not have to put on a brave face for her dearest papa. Not that she would be inclined to self-indulge in her sense of sadness but it might be revitalizing in some way to have the time to grieve a little in private for her mother, as even two years on, her bereavement process had not yet taken its full realization or course. She hated to grieve in front of her father since he was the very person who was equally grieving and although he was strong enough to carry his own engraved sadness but help her to carry hers too, she knew that he would miss her daily. However, with due consideration, perhaps it would be kind to him also, to let him complete his own healing in his own private way.

For Lord Dorchester though, it was recognition of Louise's adult independence that he was happy for her to start to make her own path in life. Perhaps an opportunity to start to understand the running of the country house would be a good start. Not only would it give her space to mentally breathe, but it might give her an opportunity to find another meaning in life. This could perhaps be an educational learning curve – delegating her with the reins of the property for a short while, might be the best thing right now. A project! So, rather than suggesting Louise take a respite from her sadness, he put it to her as a business proposal which although he suspected she would see through his idea, he also knew it would convey his absolute trust in her, as the bright woman she was becoming.

Reassurances on both parts and a firm agreement for Lord Dorchester to follow on in time for Christmas, Louise packed her cases with much improved spirit. It occurred to Louise that she had never been parted from her father since she was born – except of course for his necessary short business trips away, when she would remain at home with her mother and excitedly await his return home. Her memory flashed back to childhood images of excitedly rushing to the door upon his arrival home. Her screeches of delight were met with a powerful yet gentle bear hug as he swung her around showering her in kisses, which invariably turned into mocked eating!! "Again Papa, again!!!" she would implore him, never tiring of his attentions. The whole repeated rhapsody would inevitably end in her hiccups brought on by incessant giggles!! Such joyous homecomings!! Reflecting upon this and smiling at her own dream-like world, she suddenly felt... grown up!! A woman!!

Her father had instructed her maid Betsy to accompany her to cook and achieve all household chores in the early days, together with Jake who would take care of all heavier menial tasks and of course he would release his trusted butler Elders to offer wise advice where needed and maintain standards downstairs whilst Louise found her independent feet. He was happy to manage for himself without Elders for a few weeks, until he too arrived at Bancroft House. Rather he preferred that his daughter be in safe hands.

These staff would be sent as an advanced party to prepare the house ready for Louise's arrival some few days later. In addition, Lord Dorchester advised his daughter to advertise and employ a further few suitable staff to cover the running of the house, as she saw fit. He reminded her that she would be requiring a coachman with a stable lad for as long as she was in residence. Jimmy his own trusted and experienced coachman, would escort her to Bancroft House and return the following morning to continue in his own employ. He would at least know that his daughter had arrived safely.

Louise had had so much to think about before she left her father and she had also created lists of things to do once she had arrived at Bancroft House. She had a mind's eye view of changes she might like to consider once installed there but had never had the experience of responsibility of such budget. She wanted to prove to her dear papa, that she could make a good fist of running the house and wanted to please him with any changes she saw fit to make. She was determined not to ask for further guidance or advice but she also knew that it would be freely and kindly given if it were needed.

In the meantime, Lord Dorchester had requested to speak with his advocat of many years but learnt that he had fallen ill. However, his own son would be happy to continue advising Lord Dorchester, if he felt agreeable to this. The younger Mr. Woolmer, was now elevated to a partner in the firm and becoming very experienced in all matters. Indeed, Lord Dorchester had been impressed by the young man on the few occasions they had met and so had no hesitation in accepting his guidance on this occasion. Aged experience is one thing but sometimes a youthful eye can be equally valuable.

Sitting across the broad highly polished mahogany desk, Mr. Woolmer cast his thoughtful eye across the handwritten credentials and visibly paled. He scrutinized the detail alongside further information Lord Dorchester had furnished him with and thoroughly married up the particulars. He pored over the pages, one by one in silent concentration, then spoke with gravity. "My Lord", he paused, "It would appear that this does indeed refer to your mother!" He was caused to reflect on his own family perspicacity and muttered emphatically, "This must STOP!" Emotion thickened his voice.

Chapter 2

By the end of October, Louise and her driver Jimmy prepared to set off. If the weather was fair enough, they could make the journey in one go, stopping only for refreshment and personal comfort.

They set off as early as possible – just as daylight was breaking. Everything had been loaded up the night before – just the horses to prepare. Louise never did like to eat too much before such a long trip but about half way she was happy to dip into some light food. After some hours of uneventful travel and arriving at the Posting House in Burford, they were a little more than half way on their journey.

Routine had it that they would stop here to change the horses, at the reputable livery stables. Louise loved the approach to this building as they made that last slow drive down the tree lined hill through the centre of the village to the flat fronted building just off the main track but before the bridge over the River Windrush. Taking the opportunity at this point to alight from the carriage and stretch her legs, she breathed deeply to appreciate the air. Somehow, it smelled different. Fresher. Pure air. She smiled widely. The horses were uncoupled from the carriage, whinnying and flicking their manes as though with relief and were expertly lead away, glistening with sweat, to recuperate in the fresh hay barn. Glad of the respite, it was as though they knew Jimmy would be collecting them the next day on his way back to their home near Oxford. Louise could now tolerate peeking beneath the calico cloth of the picnic basket to discover the kindness of the housekeeper who had prepared a plentiful picnic, which could easily have fed three. She smiled to realise how much she was cared for, even by the staff. She was happy to share this bounty with her driver whom she had known all her life. Sufficiently replete, they continued their journey.

The refreshed carriage left Burford, setting off again pulling slowly up the long hill. From here on in, she knew the route quite well and followed it as best as she could, sometimes through drifts of disorientating dense mist. Reaching the elevated straighter road atop the long hill she was not able to appreciate the vast panoramic view, which normally rewarded travellers. This familiar, seemingly endless view across the Gloucestershire countryside, was today obliterated by the ethereal swirling fog, intercepted only by the late afternoon watery setting sun as it dipped lower in the darkening sky.

Onwards then towards Stow-on-the-Wold. Excitement fluttered in her stomach. Even though there was still some way to go, she felt so close to 'home' now.

The altitude and exposed position of Stow-on-the-Wold had brought wealth to this small developing market town. Silk mills had been important in its development and Louise recalled her father explaining how silk winding had become the main occupation of women and children in nearby Donnington and for the men, the brewery offered work.

As the coach rocked slowly forward through the crowds in the market square, bustling with traders and squealing animals, she peered up at the robust, square tower of St Edward's church with its splendid parapets, pondering its fine historic creation. Travel was momentarily suspended as they waited for stallholders to chaotically pack away the afternoon market. She opened the carriage window to immerse herself in the frenetic commotion of clamorous din around them. She realised that it only 'seemed' chaotic, because there was so much shouting going on but incongruously, everyone seemed to know what they were each doing: Each had a job, a task to execute. It was just that they were all doing this at the same time and with impatience, getting in each other's way! Something was knocked over in the melee and landed with a crash. A fight exploded just as the coach creaked forward and moved on. Louise closed the window and sat back in her seat, grinning.

They came across the row of almshouses. Her heart sank a little to consider those unfortunates who resided within. She simultaneously appreciated how lucky she was to have lived such a life of comfort and security. These homes held a sad intrigue for her. The inhabitants she knew, were neither insane nor criminal, yet, society had dealt them a harsh blow, for these were those poor souls who were perhaps abandoned or sick, elderly or orphaned. She reflected on how dreadful it must be to be orphaned and not to have anyone to turn to. The thought struck her hard. It was to her, unimaginable. She thought lovingly of her dear parents and wiped a single spilled tear, which had escaped onto her pale cheek.

The coach rumbled on a little across the cobbled stones, pausing now for a small herd of sheep being driven by their elderly shepherd and assisted from the rear by a pert, attentive black and white dog. The canine's sharp movements intrigued Louise, as she watched him deftly controlling the would-be disbanded sheep, in response to the repertoire of his master's whistles. Louise was fascinated in the whole procedure, transfixed by the close communication between master and dog. She had never had a dog but in that moment, she envied the close companionship one might bring.

Musing on that thought, as they continued to navigate this small frenetic scene, she glimpsed the sign of The Porch House, swinging from its post. Despite herself, Louise caught herself smiling again, as another vivid recollection was refreshed in her mind's eye. On occasion, when they were so much younger, the family trip was more often than not suspended here a brief while so that their father could engage in dialogue with an old friend. The sisters were allowed to sit demurely in the back room with their mother whilst the men stood at the bar to taste the local ale. Louise and Elspeth delighted in pointing out the witches marks upon the walls, left to ward off evil spirits. They giggled with excitement as though finding each one for the first time, even though this was a ritual game for them. They invariably begged their parents to go and seek out the tunnel, which alleged to lead from behind the bar to the church across the road but were always refused this treat, for one excuse or another. She laughed out aloud now to imagine how her father might have wished he had never told them about this piece of history!

Each turn of the road seemed to hold a childhood memory. It was quite comforting to replay the voices of her mother or father or sister as they went. She did not feel alone.

The light was getting dimmer now and together with the thickening fog, she knew she would miss the immense views as the carriage descended the steep winding hillside, which led finally to Bancroft House. She drifted in and out of sleep as the carriage swayed rhythmically down Fish Hill. By the time they reached Bancroft House, it was almost dark.

Thank goodness her staff had travelled in advance to be there to welcome her with hot food and drink. The fire roared in the grate and with tapers lit and curtains pulled closed, Bancroft House was more welcoming than it had ever been. She was glad to be here. It truly felt like home. She gratefully fell exhausted into a sumptuous bed, pre-warmed with a hot copper pan and quickly fell into a deep and relaxing sleep.

Chapter 3

Betsy Tyler yawned as she headed sleepily down the sweeping staircase towards the front parlour. One arm held shivering against her ribs as she clutched her blouse tighter round her neckline, the other hand held slightly in front of her supporting a flickering candle. She could see her own breath as she descended.

Her repeated morning routine had begun. Best just to get on with it. With a sigh, she swung open the heavy oak door into a blackened abyss and fumbled her way across the room as she had done every day since they arrived, navigating the opulent furniture towards the window casement. More than once had she stubbed her toe in a miscalculated step, straight into the front leg of the sumptuous velvet Chesterfield. Today, sufficiently conscious to remember, she managed to avoid it and clutched at the heavy, ornate fabric and dragged open a curtain. She repeated the process several times around the room until the still-dark early morning light began to permeate around the space in which she stood. Even the stars were still evident. A cold frost prickled at the mullioned glass and the early morning garden sparkled beyond.

The candle served to light other wax tapers around the room until Betsy could see clearly enough to gather what she needed, to clear the fire grate and begin her morning tasks. Well practiced now in her first chore, lighting the fire was done with alacrity and its colourful glow was rewarding even if it had not yet given forth any heat to the room. Now, to blacken the grate and polish the fire surround. The physical effort would at least serve to work up some body heat.

By the time Lady Louise had presented herself some hours later, everything would be warm, inviting and graciously welcoming. Betsy would often times reflect on how vastly different two lives could be. Her own role was seemingly born to serve. She was proud of her position as it elevated beyond her wildest dreams of achievement, yet her Ladyship by dint of birth, led what appeared to be a life of apparent upmost luxury and decadence. Lady Louise Dorchester had been truly blessed with life's good fortune. Yet Betsy knew she owed a great deal to Her Ladyship.

It was Betsy's mother who was first in her family's employ. She had worked respectfully for the family since a young woman herself. Betsy came to work with her mother from the age of thirteen, just to help during some of the busier times when there were social occasions to cater for in their stylish London town house but in fact it turned out, it was to become an unofficial apprenticeship which ultimately served her well. Her mother had become contagious after looking after a neighbour's sick child. She subsequently, sadly deteriorated in front of their eyes and having nursed the child back to health, she herself passed away. Betsy was distraught. Her Ladyship's own mother took pity on the young woman who was now left without family and kept her in their employ. Naturally this offered her accommodation too. She owed them her security and in return gave them her loyalty.

Now some eighteen years on, she found herself as the young Lady Louise's personal maid and under the guidance of her Ladyship, Betsy was capable of assisting the Housekeeper in the running of and day-to-day upkeep of their resplendent town house. Of course, she felt enormous pride to be elevated from

Lord Dorchester's household staff, to accompany Lady Louise as she set up Bancroft House but she would be more grateful when Lady Louise finally got around to employing more staff! As it stood, setting up a country home in advance of her arrival, was a daunting task with much work to be done. It had been arduous in those first few days, when everything fell on her head, from organizing food stores to cooking as well as waking up the house and cleaning. It was harder than she had bargained for! Nevertheless, Betsy rose to the challenge with her proudest foot forward! She cleared away the fire irons and stood back to admire the parlour all neat and tidy and hoped that the promised new help would soon be taking on that particular chore.

Betsy drew back the drape from one of her mistress's windows in a gentle attempt to waken her. Louise sleepily roused herself from deep slumber in the place she most thought of as home. She luxuriated in a yawn, stretching herself against the crisp linen bed sheets and turning to look through the window, she tuned into the sound of bird song. She breathed in deeply, revelling in the fresh country air and already felt rejuvenated from yesterday's journey.

Eventually rising from her warm bed, she wrapped her shawl around her shoulders and peered out through her bedroom windows. Unable to see clearly, she wiped away the moisture from the glass with her fingers to clear her aspect but gained nothing from her effort. Frustrated to see better, she cracked open the fragile casement window to expose herself to the chilly damp air. The noise disturbed a bouquet of pheasants below, causing quite a rumpus of squawking and fluttering as they scurried away in half flight. She laughed and whispered an apology to the creatures.

This, she believed, was the most wonderful view in the world. She paused to appreciate the panoramic view and heard the familiar sound of the hounds' excited barking in unison, as they were being lead out on exercise from Kennel Lane. The howling sound could carry for miles across the open countryside, more so now, with few leaves on the trees to muffle the riotous peel. She thought it a little late in the year to be hunting and so presumed they were being collectively run up Snowshill for their daily constitutional.

Bancroft House was situated at the top of the lower hillside overlooking the village of Broadway. Its glorious mellow stoned buildings and thatched roofs were the prettiest imaginable. Gentle light smoke puffed out from the chimneys, filling the morning air with that homely, familiar wood-burning aroma she so loved. In the summer, roses grew around doorways and gardens were full of fragrance. At this time of year however, when the trees were turning their leaves into golden feathers which floated on the light breeze to carpet the ground beneath and clutches of red berries were gathering on the evergreens, Louise felt it was at its best. If she looked to her left, she could easily admire Broadway Tower summiting Beacon Hill, as though within touching distance. It was incredulous to think that, with nothing much more than a whim and as the brainchild of Capability Brown, Lady Coventry had had it built upon the crest of the Cotswold Ridge, just to be assured it could be seen from her window at Croome Court! Such affluence! Yet, it was now here for Louise's enjoyment it seemed and she felt like it were her very own!

After a hearty breakfast, Louise had been so well organized before she left home, that she was able to send Jake with a pre-written note to the village store to advertise that she required a driver/stable hand, kitchen assistant and general household help. He was then instructed to also put word about as best as he could, that Bancroft House was requiring more staff. Upon his return later that day, she then employed him by re-organising a few pieces of heavy furniture in the reception rooms to make the space more convenient for her use and it was a cathartic way of starting afresh.

The garden was overgrown and would need some thought. In her quieter moments over the next few days, when the rain was lashing down outside, she would find nothing lovelier to do, than sit on the window seat overlooking the rear of the house, with a jar of hot milk and cloves and spend some hours making plans to reshape some areas. For the moment, the flowers were largely over but seed heads were so pretty that another of her joys was to browse the existing tangle of foliage and bring into the house a huge bunch of autumnal coloured leaves and grasses and arrange them in a variety of vessels around the house. Nothing more satisfying she thought, than to see the reflection of outdoor nature on a highly polished mahogany surface.

Within days of advertising, Louise was inundated with applications from young to old, many totally illiterate and all of them seemingly poor and in desperate need of work. A number of people therefore came through the doors, invited to demonstrate their skills or convince Lady Louise of their desire to work for her, from the tall and skinny to the short and rotund. From the timid to the loud. Louise heard their pleading and often pitiful stories and only wished she could have employed them all. She found the plight of many, heartbreaking and she had no idea of how she was going to make a decision. Whilst she needed people to rely on and was certainly not a charity, there were so many people out there, she realized, who were on the edge of desperation and a paid job of work could transform their lives for the better.

It was the third day of interviewing applicants and after a taxing morning, she had one more person to see before lunch. At that point, she had been shocked to have Elders escort into the room, a very timid, frail looking young woman. The girl barely looked up let alone looked Louise in the eye and she spoke mouse-quiet. She had a constant habit of nervously pulling down her ragged coat sleeves and Louise thought she caught sight of purple black bruising around her wrists – or maybe it was just filth, if her clothes were anything to go by. Her skin was dry and flakey with sores around her mouth. Poor girl looked like she hadn't had a wash or good meal in months. Louise was sure her greasy hair was infested and her own skin crawled, just a little, at the thought. Louise established her name was Rose and that she lived at home with her father, not far from Broadway. She coaxed the girl to tell her that she cooked and cleaned for him and for fear of not being able to put a meal on the table, she had at times had to resort to poaching too … Seemingly, she desperately wanted a 'proper job' and a chance to do 'Summut gud" to please her father.

Louise sat back in her chair momentarily and reflected on the comparison with her own upbringing and found a life like this in front of her, must be intolerable. The stories of resilience she had heard over the past days had shocked her. The resolve and ingenuity to survive for fear of the workhouse was gruelling and to hear of Rose's procurement of food by unlawful means was not uncommon. The desperate risk involved, had to be worth the alternative fate. Such atrocious circumstances. They were forced to be 'bricky' beyond words but Louise could not help them all!

It was anyone's guess which choices her Ladyship might make but Betsy had her own opinions of those she saw. Betsy tried her level best to extract any news from Elders but loyalty was always his code of conduct and no matter how many cups of tea and slices of cake Betsy put his way, he would not be coerced.

There was however, one day when there was rather a kerfuffle upstairs. Betsy had passed through the hallway on her way downstairs just a half hour before and seen a painfully thin young girl with straggly limp hair curtaining her shy face, being ushered by Elders into the front salon where her Ladyship was conducting her interviews. Betsy was then in the throws of making a restorative drink for Louise as her Ladyship had been busy for hours. Suddenly and without warning, the front door smashed open, allowing an icy blast of air to sweep along the downstairs hallway and causing the kitchen back door to slam with the suction of air. Betsy jumped out of her skin but on hearing a man's voice booming out angrily, she spilt the hot liquid and instinctively rushed back upstairs towards the rumpus. Elders was trying to stop a giant of a man from entering further into the hall but since the unwanted visitor was so much bigger and stronger than Elders, his efforts were futile.

'WHERE IS SHE??" He raged, "I know she's here!!! ROSE! ROSE!" He yelled fiercely, 'Get here you little witch", easily shrugging off Elders feeble attempt to grab his arm and flew at the first door he came to and banged it open. Annoyed that his hunch was wrong as he faced an empty room, his face reddened into puce as his temper angered further. "Rose I'm telling you, come here this minute or I'll beat the living daylights out of you!" he threatened.

Betsy hesitated for a split second watching this uncommon scene unfold in front of her, not knowing how to help Elders against this hulking figure but just then, the door from the Salon opened and Lady Louise appeared as graceful and calm as she could muster.

"Sir!" She exclaimed!!! "I would implore you not to shout! We are not at all deaf and welcome only civil guests." The gargantuan figure exhaled unpleasant beer-stenched breath through broken brown teeth, towards her. She flinched away in disgust. Then, bravely taking a further step towards the giant, she boldly addressed him in a quieter tone. "What is this intrusion about Sir? I will not tolerate rudeness in my home!" He began to yell again but, surprising herself, she silenced him with a flat palm towards his chest. "What is your business here?"

"That girl you have here – where is she?? She's got no right to be here. She's already got a job looking after me." In answer, Louise replied, "If by chance the girl to whom you are referring, is indeed in my home, Sir, it is because she has come here willingly. Who is she to you, Sir?"

"She's my daughter and she has no need of a job." He shouted louder, "ROSE!! Get yourself here!! Or I tell you I'll thrash you... " Louise interrupted his latest threatening rant, 'Sir!!! I will not have..." Her voice broke off as she heard behind her, the young girl appearing at the door of the salon. Her tiny frame steadily moving forward, head hanging, walked towards her father. The man pounced forward and snatched her arm. She yelped as he dragged her towards the front door.

"Sir" Louise improvised, "WAIT!" ... With no idea what words would come next, she lurched on. An instant image of her mother flashed into her head, as clearly as if she were standing there beside her ...Unscrambling her thoughts, somehow, she knew what was the right thing to do.

She began, "If you are willing to kindly allow your daughter to come and work for me here at Bancroft House, I can pay you well for her services."

He stopped in his tracks and turned.

"She will however, have to live here to fulfill her duties." ...

Rose's head slowly lifted up towards Louise with a look of incredulity and what seemed to be relief. Louise noted a purple blackness around her right eye, which was now fully visible. In an instant Louise realized that her suspicions had been accurate and that her impulsive decision was right.

"How much?" he asked greedily and without hesitation.

A deal was struck and the young girl was thus accepted into the household under the direct auspices of Betsy. Louise had agreed to pay Rose's father a fair some of money for her employ, which he would need to collect on a weekly basis from the kitchen door, provided he curbed his manners and spent a short while in Rose's company under Betsy's watchful eye. Should he cause any disturbance, the arrangement would be retracted.

In addition, Louise secretly agreed with Rose to also pay her a small amount of money which was entirely her own and which she could save or spend as she wished. Rose was completely overwhelmed with such kindness and generosity and promised Louise she would try her very best at all times.

A bed was allocated in an upper loft space, which would later be shared with the second new recruit once Lady Louise had finalized her choice. Clothes were quickly found for the girl and Betsy was under instruction from her Ladyship to have Rose put in a tub and scrubbed down.

"I'll get the Lye out your Ladyship and give her hair a good scrubbing – get rid of those hair mite!" but Louise corrected this suggestion by instructing that they dispose of any household Lye. In response to Betsy's quizzical look, she added that she did not wish the caustic fluid to burn the scalp off anyone in her care. Instead, they were all to use a beaten egg with warm water to address their hair. Betsy gave a shrug muttering something about this being a fine waste but Louise arrested the conversation by insisting this would be no inconvenience now that Jake had bought half a dozen hens at the market.

And so Rose settled in. She proved to have a slightly clumsy demeanour but Louise put this down to immaturity and above all anxious nerves. At first, she mostly observed Betsy and tried to fulfill basic tasks to assist – wiping out cupboards, washing up, collecting eggs from the yard but rarely leaving the kitchen area. She needed to learn that any mistakes made, were not going to be castigated by a sound beating. She was after all completely inexperienced but presented with a benign nature and a certain willingness to learn.

Louise's decision to take on Rose had, admittedly, been

impulsive. Neither Elders nor Betsy thought initially that this was a wise conclusion but Louise felt in her heart things would work out and considered everybody in life deserved a chance. She would have to be trained up as kitchen assistant by Betsy, who it transpired, suddenly found herself in a more senior position – and liked it!

Finally, Lady Louise had made her decision regarding the other two staff and called both Elders and Betsy into the parlour mid afternoon, to share her verdict about her next chosen member of staff, so that they could make the appropriate arrangements for their arrival.

Violet, would be joining them next week. A little older than Rose and she would be tasked to take on the role of laundry maid as well as chambermaid. Roles had to be combined at this stage, as the household was small. Violet would be responsible for any linen repair which Louise suspected would be plentiful and she had requested examples of her needlework. Violet brought in some samplers and Louise was astonished at how accomplished she was for her young age. In addition, Violet was a sweet young thing, if rather shy but kept a sensible head and seemed quick to learn.

Bearing in mind that Louise's arrangement with Rose's father and Rose herself was not regrettable, it did mean that Louise had already overspent on her tight budget. She would have to cut a financial corner somewhere else. It was also proving tricky to find a coachman AND a stable lad. Paying for an experienced coachman would prove too expensive and this was after all a small household. So by way of compromise, Louise needed someone with sufficient knowledge and understanding of the job to be successful. For the time being, Louise decided she could take responsibility for purchasing the feed and grain as long as the new employee could make sure the horses were properly fed and groomed. The new recruit would obviously require skill at driving and a general good understanding of the horses.

Eventually, she declared to Elders and Betsy that she had come across Isaac. This young man had lived all his life in the village and was currently employed as a 'mature for his young years', well respected stable hand, with a natural affinity with the horses and came with glowing references and ambition. It was a huge promotion for him but her instinct was that her gamble would pay off. She hoped!

Chapter 4

Some time in mid November, there had been a disturbance in the woodland, which ran along the upper periphery of Bancroft House land and adjacent to the neighbouring estate. Jake had gone out to firm up some of the fencing as instructed by Louise, as she had been considering buying in a small herd of cattle. The old fencing was broken down completely in parts and this would have to be attended to as a matter of priority before the spring.

Despite the ground being hard with a sharp frost and a light fog hanging in the air, the job should be started before the more severe winter weather settled in. So Jake made a start at a point some distance away from the house, where the fencing looked at its worst. It was so cold he could barely feel his hands. His fingers were entirely white, almost blue and holding the mallet was not easy. He was of slight build and the job was harder being on his own but he gave it his all, as always.

Over the course of the morning, he had successfully firmed up a number of stakes with the lengths between them and had built up quite an appetite. He was just about to sit down against the newly repaired bit of the fence and tuck in to whatever sustenance Betsy had provided that day. He hoped it was one of her homemade pies.

Quite without warning, however, a nearby gunshot rang out across the clear air and the crack of the bullet instantly spooked a flurry of birds from the trees above his head. The sound made him flinch and naturally he paused to look up. At that point, he became witness to two brawling men just inside the wooded area. Foul language permeated through the physical jumble of limbs, followed by the splat of fist on jaw as one fell with a heavy thud to the ground.

Jake's jaw dropped in fear and he turned to duck away. Catching a glimpse of his movement, the man still standing, shouted across to the apparent observer. "Oy! You!! Cum 'ere you sniveling little rat!"

Jake's head turned towards the command but hovered just a second too long. "I said cum 'ere and I means now!!" Jake, on instinct, snatched off his own cap as though in an attempt of politeness and took a slow step towards the man. "Y..yes Sir?!" he stuttered, half a question and half a reply...

Walking towards Jake, "Wot you doin 'ere?" Snapped the irritated man. "I'm fixing the fence Sir...' Jake thought to quickly add..."I didn't see anything Sir... I was just working with my head down Sir."

"Cum 'ere", the man repeated...almost growling. Jake, visibly trembling, moved towards the older man and once within arms reach, found himself grabbed by the collar and hauled up almost off his feet nose to nose with this terrifyingly angry man, the fencing between them. "You go tell your master," he snarled between his barely opened mouth, "If I find his gamekeeper on this land again, I'll kill him..." He shook Jake as though to secure the message had indeed gone though to his thick skull."

"But Sir I don't have a master!!"... wondering why he had just been so honest...The man slapped him across the face for his insolence. "Don't you give me lip yer scumbag."

"No Sir...I mean I have a mistress, Sir... I mean my Ladyship. Sir!" Exasperated, now and believing the boy to be a mutton head, "Don't be ridiculous, yer little toad. Just go tell yer Master I don't want his gamekeeper 'ere again. Understand??"

Sensing it very wise not to say more, Jake held his breath and nodded frantically with a certainty to pass on the message. That accepted, he felt himself shrugged off, as though from a great height and fell backwards into the crispy long grass.

Jake had run back to the house in a hot sweat. He arrived out of breath at the back kitchen door calling for Elders. His troubled and panicked state startled the butler who instantly noted the red mark across his right cheek and knew his request to see Lady Louise was urgent.

Not making a lot of sense, Jake babbled his story in front of Elders as Louise tried to make sense of it all. In the first instance, she was concerned for her employee's safety and that he had been subjected to threatening behaviour and physical assault, when he was rightfully on her land. She needed to find out who this aggressor was, and indeed, whoever was the man thought to be her gamekeeper, also apparently at the butt of this man's violence. She then registered her confusion at the obvious misunderstanding that anyone should think she had a gamekeeper. As if she could afford that!

When all else was considered, she then found she was irritated – even angry - at the notion that whoever this man was, he gave no credence to the notion that a woman was running the land and not a man! How dare he be so presumptuous!

She was going to have to get to the bottom of this!! Louise had, with Isaac's assistance made enquiries and managed to ascertain the name of their neighbouring landowner. Isaac knew just about everybody in and around the village and Louise got the distinct impression that from what he had heard, Isaac didn't care for this landowner's reputation. He warned Louise to be cautious about entering into confrontation with him, as he could be very nasty. With some prompting from Elders, Louise had remembered a hazy childhood image of the previous incumbent but it seems that dear old Mr. Butterworth had passed away some time ago and there had been local speculation surrounding the new proprietor. The gentleman in question, a Mr. Partridge, it was rumoured, had become wealthy through unscrupulous means and had not made his presence in the village welcome.

Louise decided a letter to this Mr. Partridge might be the right approach so she carefully crafted some firm but polite words to the effect that she did not care for his employee's threatening manner and would be obliged if, in future should he have any reason to complain, that he would have the good manners to address her personally as the incumbent proprietor of this estate.

Jake was dispatched with the letter forthwith and, still sporting a red cheek, he obeyed his Ladyship and left the security of Bancroft House with huge trepidation. By the time he reached the neighbour's mansion, his imagination had run riot and fear prickled every nerve end of his body. What if he ran into that awful man again? What if he got another beating? What if he used his gun this time? Oh God, he didn't want to be here! He wanted to turn and run in the opposite direction. He wanted somebody else to be him! He wanted to be anywhere else but here. He started to feel sick...

Louise had instructed him to be sure to give the envelope to the butler of the house. That way the message would be sure to reach the owner. Josh pushed himself to run all the way there, to get the whole thing over and done with quicker but the distance was more than he had imagined and so he expired all his energy in very little time.

Trying to reason with inner conflict, he rehearsed his instructions as he went. His plan was to run straight up to the front door, knock authoritatively, ask for the butler if he himself did not open the door and say his piece as he handed over the letter and then most appealingly, run home! The ordeal would be over before he knew it. Of course, he would not see his assailant. Why would he? He thought of Betsy's broth she was making for tea and for a moment this spurred him on, until the nausea returned.

The mansion came into view. It commanded extensive views across the village below, which nestled into the bowl of the countryside. In the distance, one could make out the Malvern Hills and in the nearer distance the town of Evesham, which seemed to spread further year on year. Jake told himself, this errand was all about a misunderstanding and would come to nothing. They would find out who their woodland intruder was and it would all be over.

The frozen gravel crunched under his shoes. His feet were dead with cold yet his body so flustered, beads of sweat appeared on his brow. He grabbed his cap off his head and scrunched it nervously in his trembling hands. The letter got carelessly crushed as he did so. Stepping up to the grand entrance he saw a bell. Tugging at the rope, he stood back a little and waited a heart stopping moment until a noise behind the façade heralded the arrival of someone. He swallowed hard. Oh god! What did he have to say again? His mind blanked. The door swung open. Somehow his tongue seemed to get stuck in his dry throat. He hopped from one limb to the other. He might wet himself. He tried to swallow.

The voice at the door spoke impatiently, "What's in your hand boy?"

No words came out from between the movement of his lips. Flustered, he went to hurriedly take a step forward to pass the envelope but his toe caught on the second step and he catapulted himself forward with a slap. Lifting only his head, he looked down to see his own blood spurting from his brow onto the stone beneath him. He passed out.

When he came to, Jake was somewhere in the back of the house with the servants. Someone, a female, had a cold cloth against his head. He looked up through vague vision and to his absolute horror, his eyes focused on a form in front of him. It was HIM!!

The man took a few steps towards Jake and bending down so that their faces were almost touching, He whispered, "Well, well, well! Look 'ere! See what the cat's dragged in!" Pausing while he moved around to Jake's side, he quietly continued in a sinisterly calm way, "So what brings you 'ere then, mmm?"

"Her Ladyship sent me... I have to deliver ....." He then realized he was not holding the letter. Panic set in. Shocked, he continued, "I had a letter" his frail voice trembled. "From Lady Louise Dorchester"... an after thought, "Sir" ...

"Did ye now?!!" ...He walked around the room. "Well where is it now then?" Jake felt like he was in the worst of nightmares. 'I don't... I don't know..." He was on the verge of tears.

"Well that's not very clever then is it?" He laughed a loud, flat laugh...

"Are ye stupid?" He spat out the words. He turned to the kitchen maid holding the bloodied cloth and sniggered his comment. "So, we have found ourselves a sniveling, little, STUPID, cry baby ... What shall we do with 'im then?? Jake certainly felt stupid! More than that though, he felt terrified!

Deliberately and with controlled voice, Jake heard him say, "What would it be worth to you, for me to find that letter then eh?? Mmm?? See, I think you'd be in a heap of trouble if that letter was lost!" Another few slow steps around the kitchen and back to Jake, he dramatically put his hand in his inside pocket and withdrew the letter, wafting it in front of Jake's nose". Jake, now ashen, gasped.

The man began again, 'See, I could make sure that this 'ere letter, gets to the Master no problem at all... "He paused for effect then whispered, "But ye first need to do me just a little favour in return..." With that, Jake winced as he gripped him by the ear and hauled him up from the chair. With one swift movement he twisted his arm behind his back and navigated him through the doorway. The body lay crumpled, partly hidden under straw in the second barn. Jake's knees threatened to buckle from beneath him. His eyes were wide with horror, as he immediately recognized the man's jacket from the wood. My God! He was dead!! He felt forceful hands behind his elbow, propelling him forward. Stating the obvious, Jake muttered more to himself than the man, 'You killed him!"

"Ha!! And I thought you were stupid!" He said sarcastically!!" Forcing Jake a little nearer, his mouth close to his ear, "You know what to do... shovel's there. Up to you 'ow you get 'im into the woods... Just do it quick, sniveler." With a menacing tone, Jake would never forget, the man added, "And if ye decide not to do it proper – or ye dare tell anyone, you'll be following 'im into a dirt grave yoursel'." With that he pushed Jake forward until he landed on top of the body.

Back in the welcoming, warm safety now of Bancroft House, Elders looked quizzically at the manservant as he entered through the back door into the kitchen. "Where in the name of all that's holy have you been lad?" asked Betsy, relieved to see Jake home again.

Chastising Jake for his tardy return, Elders asked about his bloodied forehead. Jake cobbled together a part truth about tripping up the steps but that only went part way to explaining his completely disheveled attire and late return home. Making up another cover story this time a complete lie, was the least of his worries! Having done as he had been forced to do, under the cover of early afternoon darkness, he hoped that the big man had kept his assurance about the letter. What worried Jake more, however, was the fear that he had not yet seen the last of him. A murderer. It suddenly occurred to him, that now, he himself was an accomplice to the crime. Oh God!!

Chapter 5

Wiilliam Partridge opened the scrunched letter and read the words before him. It was as though a piece of litmus paper had been lit. Slamming his fist on the table before him and with an explosion of filthy language, he called for his quivering butler to drag Thunder to him immediately.

As soon as the door opened and the huge man had barely entered, Partridge began his tirade, heaping upon his lackey a torrent of abusive criticism and threats.

"What the hell were you doing out there for me to get this letter? Are you completely mad drawing attention to me like this, you stupid heap of mutton! You're no more use to me than a bag o'misery!!! I don't know why I give you stable space, you good for nothing idiot of all idiots. You're nothing but a waste of space – that's what you are!!! Didn't I tell you to deal with that snooping detective without causing a fuss? Well, didn't I?" He did not require an answer. "You blithering fool – you start waving that gun around for all to hear and now I've got Madam Upstart on my heels!"

As far as he was concerned, anything that his lackey had to say for himself was a waste of time anyway. Not that Thunder was trying to answer! He knew of old, he would be wasting his breath. So he stood silently, taking all the tongue lashing, verbal insults he'd heard many times before. Continuing his ranting, "Who in God's name does she think she is? – Jumped up haughty wench!" Getting it off his chest, his diatribe was to nobody in particular, "The audacity of her to write to ME to tell ME how to behave!! Where has this temerity come from Thunder? What happened out there? I'll not have her speak to ME like this" he fumed, waving the letter in the air above his head. His cathartic outburst continued, "Been here five minutes she has, without her father, and thinks she owns the place. Well, nobody speaks to me like this!! The nerve of it!!! She needs teaching a lesson," he bawled as he turned on his heels to face Thunder, nose to nose. "And you're going to be the one to do it!!! Get yourself over there and drag her out by the hair if you have to! You get her here... d'you understand, idiot???" He considered his choices, "The workhouse is too good for her. No, I think she might have other qualities! Thinks she's posh, does she?? Well, we'll see about that! I need to give here a decent talking to! Suddenly inspired, he added, " – or more!!" Turning to face a mottled mirror on the wall, he preened himself, then laughed a filthy laugh. "I'll enjoy that!"

He turned quickly on his heels and snapped his final warning, "Find out when she'll next be on her own and you get her. Understand! You bring her here. D'you think you can manage that without mucking it up?" he questioned sarcastically. "Now, get the hell out of here!" Thunder was dismissed.

This was a different job Thunder had been given and he was a little anxious. It seemed to involve going into the neighbour's house to achieve his goal. His usual assignments were to scoop up from the streets. He manhandled orphans or abandoned children or those who were mentally sick or disabled and deliver them to Broadside Workhouse. Their strength against his was easily managed. They didn't usually give him much of a challenge. Sometimes, however, he took unmarried mothers. He liked these bawdy wenches because there was usually a bonus to be taken, if he was lucky. He liked to make them plead

and scream and scratch. He took their babies as enticement –
he learnt quickly that a mother would do anything to protect
her child. He learnt faster that you didn't even have to keep
promises either. Babies were just a nuisance and could not be
put to work for years so he found it more convenient to 'lose'
the baby on the way, once their purpose was fulfilled. Other
times, he'd wrestle with resistant, feisty old people who were
really too weak to ever win against his strength but he had
become adept in taunting them until they reached their utmost
distress. So satisfying!

He would however, need to give this job, greater thought.

Chapter 6

It was mid December. Snow had been threatening all day with the odd flakes swirling past the windows and there was an icy blast whenever the doors had been opened. The morning had never seemed to get lighter and Elders had instructed Jake to make sure the downstairs fires had been kept stoked.

It was some time past midday when the front door knocker purposefully resounded into the marbled hallway. Moments lapsed. The sharp footsteps of the butler strode with determined composure towards the arched door and peeled back its heavy weight. Before him, quite unexpectedly, there stood an exceptional sight. There was a flurry of movement upon the third step down but his first gaze lay upon a fine gentleman. Appearing perhaps of some thirty years, exquisite attire, tall, upright stature – a stranger to the doorstep. Another movement – something hiding behind the gentleman... Lowering his gaze, Elders realized it was ...a child. Large chestnut eyes peeped from behind the stranger's tailcoat, then disappeared again, hiding.

'May I assist you Sir?" offered Elders, realigning his gaze towards the gentleman.

Momentarily distracted by the child's antics, the gentleman focused himself upon the butler. "I am not expected and for that I apologise Sir but I am here to request an audience with Lady Louise Dorchester", he stuttered.

Quickly trying to make sense of the scene and a thousand

questions rushing through his head, Elders needed time to assess the gentleman's extraordinary request. Anybody of any breeding would have forwarded an earlier request before arrival. This raised concern in Elders' mind. Yet, noticing a crested carriage, rocking slightly on the gravel driveway behind them as the horses fidgeted, alleviated his immediate concern.

Hesitating for a moment, Elders took note of the now thicker fall of snowflakes resting on the unexpected couple and not wishing to maintain a draught in the hallway, decided to ask the gentleman to step inside and of course the little girl, like a limpet, entered too. They were to excuse the butler for a few moments to see if 'Her Ladyship' was available to accept guests.

The fireplace welcomed them with its roaring warmth and orange-red glow. The gentleman dusted off his shoulders to rid the now wet melted flakes and simultaneously glanced around the room he found himself in. In the butler's absence, he chided the little girl. "Izzy!!!" He hissed quietly. "Please leave go of my tails!! You will succeed in wrecking my fine coat!!! The little girl, more from intrigue than taking instruction, loosened her grip as her eyes wandered around the sunlit foyer. Incredulous to her surroundings, her jaw fell open in astonishment. She had never seen such beauty. She had never imagined it existed. Her eyes fell upon one artifact after another, holding them in her sight for moments as though to absorb every detail. She was just studying a piece of taxidermy, transfixed trying to understand its lifelessness, when the door across the room swung open and jolted her from her reverie...

Louise's purposeful stride from the parlour into the hall seemed to falter as her eyes set upon the unexpected stranger... With almost indiscernible hesitation, "Good afternoon Sir!" Louise managed to greet her unknown guest before her words were to dry up. Catching her breath at the sight of this handsome form before her, she seemed to take an age to drag away her eyesight from his most attractive appearance and compose herself enough to fix eye contact, "Forgive me Sir, I do not seem to recognize you! How may I be of assistance?" she suddenly stammered. The pit of her stomach seemed to melt as he responded – a rich, deep, mellow voice which belied his young years ... So entrancing was the voice that she had at first no idea what he had just said. She found herself however, responding to his handshake and realizing she had already missed his name, with some quick thinking, she stirred herself ... "Oh, how rude of me! Forgive me! I see there is a carriage outside – you must have travelled some distance! Please... come and take a seat by the fire whilst we talk."

Turning to the butler, "Elders, fetch some refreshments for our visitors immediately." She turned and led the unlikely couple into the parlour where a roaring fire welcomed them and gestured for them to take a comfortable seat. 'Now, let us start again!" she invited.

The gentleman remained standing however: "Madam, firstly, please accept my apologies for this intrusion. I am not in the habit of arriving unannounced and I thank you for your hospitality. We have indeed travelled some distance and I am sure my erm... young companion would be grateful for your offer of a drink!" He cast a glance towards the seemingly shy little girl, who looked self consciously downwards at her boots as he spoke." Louise noticed the little girl's hands clasped in front of her coat. A fleeting cognizance. Curiosity momentarily took her attention. These were not the hands of a cosseted child of the apparent status of her male companion. Her skin looked damaged, sore and rough skinned.

She returned her gaze to the gentleman and as though beginning afresh, the guest resumed his train of thought and raking his fingers through his jet black hair, reiterated his original introduction. Louise fought against the distraction of noting how a forelock naturally fell back unrestrained across his handsome brow. "As I said, my name is Tobias Henry Woolmer" and turning once again to gesture towards the little girl, "...and I would like to introduce Izzy... That is, Isabella Constance Woolmer".

Tobias nudged the little girl gently and inclining his head with a nod towards Louise as though to remind her of her manners. Izzy hesitated then slowly stood in a rehearsed manner and without eye contact, gave a very clumsy, wobbly curtsy towards Louise. With a rush she then returned to Tobias's side. Tobias smiled –such a generous smile she mused – and nodded his approval before returning his attention once more to Louise.

"Well in return, I ask you to please forgive my appalling manners for not introducing myself correctly – I am Lady Louise Dorchester, but I assume you must already know this?" I admit to being curious, Sir, as to the reason for your visit!"

Louise held out her hand and without hesitation he reciprocated the gesture by gently holding her tiny fingers in his for just moments, "Delighted to make your acquaintance Madam" he offered politely, catching her gaze for what seemed like an eternity. Louise withdrew her hand and turned to the little girl adding, "I am delighted to meet you too, Izzy". Izzy flushed bright red and froze but finding rare confidence, she too stared deeply into Louise's sea green eyes as though transfixed, her mouth gaping just a little. In that moment, Louise mentally acknowledged the likeness between them.

Again, Louise re-invited them to be seated. Elders arrived with a tray of refreshments – carrot beer for the adults and a glass of warmed milk for Izzy. In addition, a plate of freshly baked cakes and biscuits. Izzy's eyes grew wide open and her mouth, followed suit!

Louise was touched to see how this Mr. Woolmer attended to the child, guiding her in good manners as he assisted her with her drink and chosen cake. Equally, it was heartwarming to see how the child hung on his every word and followed his instruction impeccably.

Thanking Louise for her unexpected but appreciated kindness and hospitality, he tried to hastily get to the point of his visit. Clumsily he burst forth with an all too brief, factual resumé of the purpose of his 'errand'. It amounted to loosely explaining that he had unexpectedly accepted temporary wardenship of Izzy until he had managed to locate a suitable guardian and through his revered client, Lord Thomas Dorchester, Louise's father, he had found the perfect person in Louise!!!.... He had therefore escorted the child for her safeguarding. The whole short dialogue was overly clinical and matter of fact and Tobias had finished before Louise's brain could even rationalize his words...

Louise shook her head in disbelief whilst Tobias spoke, as though to negate his outlandish words. Suddenly realization of his sincerity dawned and as though in slow motion, she sprang to her feet with almost a shriek, "No! There is a mistake...You are in jest, surely? I don't unders...? I... But you cannot..." In that split moment, she quickly bit her tongue remembering decorum as she became conscious that this was not a conversation to be had in front of the young child. Louise bethought her hasty reply and in a hurried reflex movement, she reached for the butler's bell pull next to the fireplace, yanking it in almost panic. She silently paced between the window casement and the fireplace, wringing her hands in worried disbelief.

As soon as Violet opened the door in response to her call, Louise snapped an instruction to bring Rose. The room and her guests remained silent. Moments later a nervous, red face arrived at the door and bobbed a curtsy. Terrified she had done something wrong, Rose was visibly relieved to hear her mistress request she escort Izzy into the kitchen and maybe if Purrcillus was to be found, to allow her to feed the cat some milk... Izzy jumped to her feet smiling widely showing her lack of two front teeth, as though all her happy days had come at once and glancing briefly at her companion for permission, immediately followed the young maid beyond the door, which was softly closed behind them.

Turning now to her guest, "Forgive me" Louise began with incredulity, ...Her eyebrows raised in sceptical question "I seem to have somewhere misunderstood your words..." Louise continued to pace the room. Tobias also stood. "Oh please sit down Mr.... erm Woolmer" she snapped. "Are you seriously suggesting that ...out of the blue... you would expect me to take charge of a young girl... just like that?? A child I know nothing about? In fact... I don't know anything about CHILDREN!! I don't know anything about YOU!!!"...

"Madam, I can understand this has come as a huge shock to you but.."

"SHOCK????!! HA!! That Sir is an understatement! You understand nothing!! This is absurd!!! If this suggestion is a serious proposition, (which I cannot believe it is!) ... do you not think Sir, that this would have been dealt with differently? ...That my father would first have discussed this with me? ... That my lawyer would have not contacted me in advance? ... This is outrageous! You simply cannot expect to turn up unannounced at my door and tell me I now have to care for an unknown child! No! I won't have this", she scoffed loudly "... It is simply too preposterous for words. I must ask you to take the child and leave!!"

Baffled at this tirade, "Madam." He began – imploring her with a gesture, as though he did not know what words would follow.... "Please... might I try better to explain this bizarre interruption to your peaceful day..."

"Sir! I can't possibly see how there could be ANY explanation of this farcical intrusion!" Feeling panicked, "No! You must take your leave immediately!" Louise once more strode towards the bell pull and hastily tugged at it. It seemed like she would have to wait an eternity for Elders to respond. She needed to get this madman out of her home. She was shaking almost uncontrollably with shock or even outrage but mostly she believed, with fear.

Then it was her guest who paced the room before stuttering another apology. Louise was staggered at his imposition to be still there present, invading her hospitality but at the same time intrigued and something made her want to at least listen to any explanation he may have to offer. Her legs suddenly felt weak with reaction to the whole disturbance and with a frustrating sigh, she sank heavily into her leather desk chair.

Mr. Woolmer meanwhile shaking his head, also in disbelief, then tried to speak words to make sense of this entirely bizarre moment, "Madam..."

Fidgeting anxiously, wringing his hands in stunned desperation to hold his own attention, he reeled with shock and bewilderment at her wholly vehement reaction. He mentally scrambled together words to try to reasonably explain his plight and so, he began again, in a firm, businesslike manner. "Having spoken to your father, I took this opportunity today to visit you, as it was the first chance I had to travel amidst my work commitments. In that respect, I appreciate the suddenness of this intrusion and I repeat my apologies." He rushed his words until he was now gabbling, "However, I am now flabbergasted beyond words to be under the strong impression that you are in no way prepared for this?"

A barely audible knock at the door broke Mr. Woolmer's train of thought and brought Louise back to the present from this nightmare like scenario. "Yes Ma'am?" questioned Elders. Louise glanced up and spoke more calmly, "Bring me the brandy and two glasses, Elders, if you will."

"Yes, Ma'am, of course." Elders retreated curiously and softly closed the door. Louise appeared for that moment, to be resigned to listen, Mr. Woolmer continued. "I was totally under the impression that your father had discussed this matter with you and..." Words failed the man, as he exuded a hefty sigh. He was not only shocked at Louise's fervent response but also befuddled beyond words and deeply embarrassed. Shaking his head in disbelief, he tried to make sense of this entirely bizarre moment. "Madam..." He began again, raising his hands with a questioning shrug, "I don't understand! Have I clearly miscalculated this?" He could not believe he had, yet struggled to fathom sense out of this ludicrous encounter...

A deep breath to calm his voice and remembering he had prepared a speech a hundred times, it had not ever occurred to him how difficult this might be in reality! Finally, without any relation to the words he had rehearsed and with a barely audible voice, he began...

"It was five years ago, my beautiful sister Sarah – older than myself and someone I grew up adoring, was to be married. They were very much in love – anyone could see that". He paused as though controlling more emotion than he cared to show. "They were a week away from the wedding – all preparations in place and our whole household was so excited for her special day. I had never seen her so happy!"

Louise, almost impatiently, wondered where all of this was going and shuffled a little in her chair. Her frown prompted him to continue, however hard this was going to be.

"We had gathered at our parents home to discuss final details for the day of the ceremony and were about to go into dinner. We had waited a little while for Jonathan, Sarah's fiancé and decided he would have to catch us up once the meal was served." He smiled, remembering: "He was never very prompt and we thought little of it. Our meal long since finished and Sarah was beginning to look concerned. It had grown dark. Jonathan had been hosting a shoot at Montford House, his country pile some miles away – the home where he would take his bride after the wedding to begin their future together." He knew he was digressing but not realizing it was a cathartic release to talk his thoughts out aloud, he quietly continued.

"We tried to calm Sarah's increasing agitation but truth be told, we were all becoming anxious as to why he may be so delayed. It must have been about midnight when a resounding knock came to the front door. We all seemed to know it would be bad news. Moments passed although seemingly an age before the butler, grave faced, came into the front parlour where we had remained waiting. He did not need to say a word. A sombre look towards my father as he tried to clear his throat but words did not come forth from his lips and succeeded only in looking at the floor unable to speak. It was quickly evident that Jonathan had met his fate. Nobody spoke. Sarah collapsed. None of us could focus.

'What had happened?' interrupted Louise, unwittingly absorbed in this stranger's story.

"Jonathan had been involved in a shooting accident. They had tried to save him but ... the bleeding was just too much. There was nothing they could do."

"I'm so sorry, Sir" she said as sympathetically as anyone could, "but how does this ...???" She stalled.

"Yes. Of course" He anticipated. "I'm sorry... it is important that I explain as fully as I can the circumstances which bring me here", he stuttered.

"Sarah was in a terrible state of grief for weeks as I'm sure you can imagine" he continued. She took to her bed. She cried incessantly. Heartbroken, she barely had the strength to attend his funeral – but pallid and weak as she had become, she did so. Over the weeks that followed, we all thought her continuing malaise was excessive grief. We failed to help her no matter how hard we tried."

He sat momentarily. Louise relaxed into his voice, realizing how hard this must be for him to tell this story. A tender feeling swelled in her chest.

Resuming his composure, he persevered. "One day some months later, I was visiting her – as I tried often as possible to do. Suddenly, she took me by the hand and said that something wonderful but at the same time terrible had happened to her. She floundered to try to bring forth her words as though she almost dare not speak them. She had found herself with child. Jonathan's child. What a wonderful gift – yet … such shame came with this knowledge and she felt sick at the thought that she would be cast out from society for her 'indiscretion'. A child out of wedlock would bring SUCH shame it would be intolerable. How cruel."

Suddenly, the realization hit Louise. "This child…" She stuttered… "Is it Izzy??"

"Indeed Madam." There was still much to tell. He felt compelled to explain it all.

Louise began to piece together some of the story which was unfolding before her. Still very much unsure how this had come to her door was at the forefront of her mind but she grew more patient to listen.

Elders knocked and entered the room in one gentle motion, placing the tray on the side table. Louise gestured for him not to pour. He left immediately.

Tobias sighed: A deep and weary depth of sorrow. "Sarah was sent away to an elderly Aunt's home miles away and kept confined for the remaining months so that her secret was held private for as long as possible. Mother and father were wonderful really but they knew only too well the humiliation that this would bring on the whole family, should her condition be discovered."

"Eventually, Izzy was born. I don't know too much about these things but I remember Sarah shedding many tears through her pregnancy and I am told it had been a difficult birth. Sarah was damaged and exhausted. However, she had succeeded in bringing forth such a beautiful child into the world."

Louise interjected from her silence, "So I assume she had not been allowed to keep the child?"

"It was altogether not so simple" Tobias responded. "Sarah had been insistent throughout her days of confinement, on keeping the child – it was, after all her last link with her beloved Jonathan - or at least have contact with her growing up. However, Izzy never seemed to settle. Perhaps it was, as Sarah herself thought, that her continued malaise made it impossible for the tiny child to sleep or feed. Sarah cried through day and night – and so did Izzy. The child could not feed properly and Sarah was accused by our Aunt of this being her fault because she had been a 'wicked girl' bringing a child into the world out of wedlock."

Louise's face fell with horror at the poor girl's predicament. She gestured for her gentleman visitor to continue.

"This in itself broke Sarah's heart, for she truly loved Jonathan. Izzy became more and more hungry and suffered from the gripes. Sarah refused a wet nurse but finally gave in to the doctor's recommendation of a gripe remedy to settle the baby. Still too young for arrowroot, baby was administered surfeit water."

Louise was familiar with this remedy - the strained off juice from a mix of brandy and mature poppy leaves, tasted with sweet liquor and water.

"It brought little respite to the tiny babe. Sarah herself became highly aggravated by sleep deprivation – not just because of the baby but also it seems she had contracted puerperal fever after the birth. She would writhe with pain and grew thinner by the day. Sarah grew irrational and began to believe that perhaps the baby's petulance was because she had not yet had her christened."

"Unfortunately, our cantankerous Aunt was far from a compassionate woman and venomously warned Sarah repeatedly of the likelihood that she would be ridiculed in church during the service because her child was born in fornication."

Louise gave an audible gasp to hear of such cruelty. But Tobias resumed his train of thought.

"Nevertheless, the local vicar was brought in to discuss the baptism but sadly, he too accused her of being ungodly." Tobias reflected on this for a moment, shaking his head almost in disbelief!

"Sarah became so distraught that her sanity seemed to fail her. Seeing no other option, one morning, she decided to take the child's life and planned then to take her own. So, overwhelmed with grief, shame and exhaustion, she took a pillow to the child's face. Sobbing so loudly that her distress reached the ears of a passing chambermaid. Bursting into the room, Sarah's act was thankfully interrupted by the maid and Izzy's life was saved. Sarah collapsed with weary distress."

"Izzy was thus sent in haste and without consideration to a local wet nurse for a small reward. Having the baby snatched from her, Sarah lost all control. Screaming and ranting, thrashing and pacing, the Doctor deemed her quite mad and said he had no choice but to have her admitted to a lunatic asylum."

Tobias had had no previous plan to divulge such private matters but, finding himself lulled into such uninterrupted dialogue, it had proved so purgative that he found it difficult to refrain from every painful detail. He paused for some moments and strode towards the window as though gasping for air and took several deep breaths. Over and over again.

Louise quietly moved forward and poured a small brandy, placing it in front of her visitor. Nodding his acknowledgement, he swallowed the amber liquid in one. Louise took his elbow and gestured him to sit once more. She too sat. Finally, "How terrible for her – and for you Sir," she found herself whisper.

With immense courage he spoke again. "I saw her. Just the once. It was horrific..." - He gripped at his empty glass. The muscle in his jaw twitched. "The stench.... She looked unrecognizable. The pain from her birth injuries was no longer endurable for her. They chained her up – 'for her own safety.'"

He sniggered to himself in disbelief. "She begged me to help her die." He snatched his breath and held it for a moment before he swallowed hard. "She was not mad, madam.... She was so very sick and...." Another seemingly interminable pause, followed by a desperate expulsion of words, "I couldn't help her." He slammed his fist hard on the table before him and growled with pitiful emotion, "I DIDN'T HELP HER!!!"....

Louise jumped at the sound. Her heart swelled to see such pain in a man. It reminded her of her father at her mother's graveside. She thought she would never see such pain again. Louise knew there would only be one ending to this story. Tobias saw compassionate understanding in her face as he stared back into her darkened eyes, then nodded, confirming what she had rightly guessed.

"She died two days later".

Chapter 7

Moments lapsed. Both Louise and her visitor had fallen silent. Finally, Louise gently broke the stillness, "What happened to Isabella?"

A sharp intake of breath prepared Tobias for his next painful memory. "Our aged Aunt saw no reason to take any responsibility for the newborn and so my parents saw fit for the wet nurse to keep her and raise her in return for a modest fee and the agreement that my parents could visit the child from time to time. My mother would use these visits to take treats for the family and ensure Izzy was being treated as well as they hoped and kept safe." He paused in an effort to focus his mind and keep the explanation concise...

"Times were hard." He glanced towards her, briefly, "If you remember the drought in these parts a few years ago and poor crops brought greater poverty than usual. One day when my mother visited, Izzy had already gone, as had the other children."

Another pause..."It took months and months to find her. It seems that due to her very young age, she had been sent from workhouse to workhouse and finally ended up at a place some considerable miles away, in a stench ridden factory, picking oakum." It suddenly dawned on him and added as an aside, "In fact, I believe not too far from here!" He winced to consider the God forsaken place he found her in. "Izzy was just so very small and had been passed from pillar to post because nobody could stop her crying – it didn't matter how hard they beat her, she still cried. Of course she did!!" His jaw clenched as he stuttered on.

"She missed the 'family' that she knew. At least they were kind to her and fed her. Her home had been basic but ...these places are terrible. She was frightened – terrified! She wet herself constantly and being so weak, had little strength to do any task asked of her – so they beat her again."

Louise made to move towards him but he flinched and turned slightly away. "I found her filthy ... sitting on a cold stone floor surrounded by slightly older children, all dressed the same in ill fitting rags. All with that same look – an utterly despondent, hopeless, fearful, empty look. They were all tasked to do the same. The cast ropes from the ships were brought in for them to undo. The children got the last part of the unpicking, so with their tiny fingers they could shred the finest threads into softer fibres. These threads are still full of tar, salt, grit and their hands often bled. They could barely use their hands at all but knew if they halted, there would be a thrashing.

Izzy did not know me but I recognized her only by that same haunting, pleading look her mother cast me on my last visit. In that moment I pledged to myself two things:

Firstly, since I believe I had failed Sarah, I would not fail this child. Like many other children there, she did not deserve to be treated like an animal. She did not warrant the beatings, the indignation and the tortuous work. She deserved a childhood such as her mother and I had had.

Secondly, whoever was responsible for such prolific inhumane treatment in this workhouse, for their own personal gain, would be brought to justice and places like this would be criminalized. I swear, if it is the last thing I do, it will be to find that person – that beast, and put him in prison never to be released!!"

Louise's heart melted. She was mesmerized by this stranger's story and instantly warmed to his compassion. Just the resonance of his voice was entrancing enough but to listen to his version of events, which had brought him to her door, was deeply moving. She had wanted to stretch out her hand to rest on his and comfort his emotional pain.

It seemed that many silent moments passed between them.

With a pause of slow heartbeats, she eventually looked him in the eye and drawing a deep breath, began..."Sir!".... she started abruptly. She took another deep breath then exhaled with a sigh. "Mr. Woolmer"... she recommenced, more softly this time... "It is with great respect that I speak these words. Your narratives are spellbinding – indeed heart breaking – and I am deeply moved by your desire to find your niece a secure and happy home. In fact I feel honoured that you feel you could entrust me to be her guardian, but Sir, I have to remind you that I am completely removed from this scenario and have no link whatsoever with you or this child. I have no idea why my father might have put forward my name to you – or even considered it! I have even less notion why he would not have mentioned this to me in any case." She paused reflecting on this last sentence, somewhat baffled, then added, "I have no understanding of children, nor do I wish to have!"

A deep breath then to the point, "I have to ask you to leave now Sir and take Izzy with you to find a home somewhere else where she can be happy. Perhaps with other children..." A slight hesitation and with no more to be said, Louise stood and Tobias followed suit.

Nodding acceptance and respecting her decision, he stretched out his hand to thank Louise and with a heavy heart suggested that the child be brought to him. Louise hated the awkward few moments which passed between them, whilst they waited for Rose to return the child to the parlour. She tried to fill the embarrassing lull, by asking Tobias from where he had travelled and staccato small-talk dialogue then ensued.

Finally, Rose brought a very excited Izzy back into the room desperate to tell her uncle all about her adventures with the maid and Purrcillus. Tobias interrupted her chatter with his forefinger against his lips as a signal to stop. At that moment, Elders followed in with their cloaks.

Elders caught Louise's eye and nodded towards the casement window behind her. Louise turned. "Oh my goodness!" She exclaimed. I had no idea the snow had become so thick. "I do hope your journey will be safe, Sir!" She added, concerned.

"I'm sure we shall be fine My Lady. I think we shall no doubt call by The Eight Bells Inn and secure a hot meal before we return home. Once again, please accept my apologies for our uninvited interruption into your day and might I thank you profusely for your kind hospitality."

Smiling her acknowledgement, Louise escorted them into the hall for their departure. Tobias reminded Izzy of her manners and the little girl again tried out her attempt to curtsy, this time a little more confidently and thanked Lady Louise for her kindness, adding "I really liked Purrcillus ....and Rose!!" She grinned her appealingly toothless grin.

Elders swung open the door to reveal a white curtain of blustering snowflakes. Tobias bent to scoop up the little girl in his arms and with a final goodbye, carefully trod the steps and into the awaiting carriage. The neighing horses set off with the carriage slipping erratically behind them. A perilous wintry journey lay ahead of them as they attempted the short but steep ascent of the hillside, before dropping downwards in the direction of Chipping Campden.

Elders closed the heavy door and turned to note a look of uncertainty creeping across his Ladyship's face as she retreated to the parlour, requesting a pot of tea be delivered to her fireside table. With that, Elders was dismissed but since he had known her since childhood, she could hide very little from him. He intuitively knew something was deeply troubling her and was certain it was not simply her guests leaving in perilous weather.

Chapter 8

Days prior, Lady Louise had called her staff together. She had wanted to reward them for their hard work since they had arrived at Bancroft House just a few weeks ago and had suggested a special treat of an afternoon off duties, to do as they pleased. She would add in a few coins in their pockets to enjoy whatever they chose to do.

Apart from Betsy, all four of them agreed to go to watch a skating competition, at the side of the lake, along the road track into the village not far from Bancroft House.

As the gentleman and little girl left that snowy afternoon, heading towards the small neighbouring town, the staff realized that the air was bitterly cold and snow was falling thickly. Despite this, there was a sense of anticipation amongst them, even though they were beginning to wonder if the event might be cancelled. Even so, they decided they would set out anyway and see what happened. They had been talking about it for days and couldn't possibly waste such an exciting opportunity.

Louise had not had a good afternoon. Her mind was spun with conflicting thoughts. Her feminine instinct almost hurt at the stories Tobias had retold about this little girl's short life and his compassionate imploring for her to take on this young child as her guardian. All this, on top of her own struggle with grief and her intended plans to enhance the running of Bancroft House and make her father proud of her. Then, of course, there was the notion that her father had said nothing to her about this in the first place – Why would he do that??? This must have been spoken of weeks ago!! Her mind was a whirl of questions without answers. She went over and again, the dialogue she had had with Tobias – and then there was 'that feeling' she had in the pit of her stomach when she thought of him – why would her stomach flip when she pictured him?

Nevertheless, Louise tried to deal with the paperwork she had been dealing with before her visitors had arrived. She found concentration particularly hard. She realized she had developed a headache and was not in the mood for Betsy's fussing about her not eating. She had not realized how snappy she had been with her maid – which had raised Betsy's eyebrows on more than one occasion.

Louise had never taken on so much responsibility and needed to be sure that her father's allowance was being used sensibly and wisely. She had struggled over some accounts until her headache worsened as the afternoon progressed. She was desperate for sleep, so decided to take herself off to bed early.

She had given Betsy permission to take the evening off to join a small group of women in the village hall who met once a month to do crafts. For the last two months, they tasked themselves to make children's clothes for a Christmas charity. The clothes would be distributed to the poor on Christmas morning. The village hall was not very far from Bancroft House so Betsy planned to later have an early night herself. Elders would be there, as always, if she needed anything.

Before she left, Betsy had made sure the heavy drapes were all pulled closed to keep the window frosts from chilling the room. She had stoked the fires and taken a hot bed warmer to put between the sheets in Louise's big bed. She made Louise a hot milk to set aside her bed, just as her mother would have asked her to do.

Louise slipped into bed and closed her eyes, willing away

her sore head. She needed sleep! An image of Tobias and Izzy instantly came into her mind.

Tobias had gently settled Izzy onto the leather seat of the carriage as it started forward on the slippery road. He questioned his sanity making the trip in such inclement weather as the coach slipped perilously up Fish Hill, making slow progress forward – in fact, he concluded, he had been completely mad to make the journey at all! What an idiot he had been, to think that a complete stranger would take a child just on hearsay of her father's recommendation. He had been too impetuous! He should have written first. He should have had documentation. He should have assured himself that Lord Dorchester had indeed spoken to his daughter first. He should have... He scraped back his hair in his habitual way and flopped back in the seat with self disgust... What an idiot!!! He thought to himself, suddenly feeling exhausted. Talking to Louise about the past, had he realized, completely drained him of all emotional energy. He had spoken about details he had allowed to lay dormant for years and addressing them today had refreshed all that pain, as though he had just relived everything all over again.

Izzy missed nothing!! "What is the matter uncle Tobias?" She looked at him with those doe eyes that melted his heart.

"Oh nothing for you to worry about dear child. Everything is fine!" Turning the subject, "Are you hungry?"

Izzy was always hungry!! She nodded, as he knew she would.

It was obvious to Tobias that the driver was struggling to maintain a steady pace and he recognized the roads were becoming more dangerous as the carriage slipped erratically. It was clearly unwise to go much further, so only a few minutes from leaving Bancroft House, he decided to arrest their journey as soon as possible. Izzy screeched with excitement as Tobias shouted instructions up to the driver. Izzy thought she was having the best day ever!!

Always having something to say, Izzy chatted on again, "Uncle Tobias" she began, "I really like that lady. She is so pretty is she not?" He looked at his niece to confirm, "Lady Louise? Yes, indeed she is!" replied Tobias truthfully. Before he had chance to change the subject again, Izzy added, "I liked her daughter too!! Rose was funny and she let me play with Purrcillus and feed him milk!!"

Smiling, Tobias continued the dialogue, "I'm glad you had fun Izzy but Rose is not that lady's daughter – Rose is the maid."

"Oh!" Izzy looked perplexed. "But Rose lives there, Uncle Tobias – I thought ... well where is Rose's mamma then??"

"I don't know Izzy." Tobias was trying to keep this brief. He was too tired for this kind of exchange but Izzy continued with her intrigue, "Or, perhaps she's like me without a mamma?"

"Everybody has a mamma, Izzy. We've talked about this before haven't we? Everybody has a mamma and a papa – but they don't all live with us. Some have gone to Heaven – like your mamma and papa." Izzy chipped in, "But my mamma and papa still love me don't they?" He looked at her lovingly, "Your mamma loved you so very much Izzy and I believe she always will. Your papa too, would have adored you!"

Reaching across the carriage, he whispered teasingly, "And now I love you more than anybody in the whole wide world!!!" Before his words had finished, he started to tickle her until she giggled so much she could barely breathe....., saved only by the coach coming to an abrupt halt.

Tobias opened the carriage window to better communicate with his driver, who shouted down his concerns to his master, advising him that the weather had become too difficult to navigate the road safely. It was insane to even try to reach the intended Eight Bells Inn at Chipping Campden and proposed they stop at the very next opportunity. Tobias, of course, agreed.

Chapter 9

Violet in particular was SO excited. She loved to watch skating and hoped that, one day, she would be able to learn. There was no way that she could even think of owning her own pair of skates, even if she saved really hard but she could dream all the same!

This was not the only reason though, that she was so excited. Jake would be there too – naturally. Her best wish ever, would be that he spoke to her about something other than work. She fantasized about what he might say. Or he might even ask her something? "Oh Heavens! I hope I don't get flustered and get tongue-tied," she suddenly thought. She would then begin to imagine all the possible things he might ask her, so that she could have a ready reply. She wanted so badly to seem smart and attractive and interesting so that he would want to find out more about her. He would need to know all about her family perhaps – That would be fine, except she wouldn't have to mention about her brother. He'd been in trouble with the police and that wouldn't seem good. A potential beau might not like that! ... So, she would not lie but just not mention him! That would be ok, she thought.

Then she wondered if she ought to ask him something about himself? That's how it worked isn't it? Her friend Josie had told her so. She was older and wise... so ...she must think of some questions to ask him surely... but what could she ask? After some consideration, she decided, "Where do your parents live?"... or "Do you have any brothers or sisters?" That's good!! She approved of herself and felt proud of herself for coming up with such questions!

More confident now that she felt prepared, she paid attention to how she wore her bonnet and wished she had a fine coat to wear and that her gloves were not repaired time and again. Nobody could ever call Violet pretty but this was her lot and she accepted sadly that her clothes were 'serviceable' and clean. As she brushed her hair, she whispered to herself, practising asking an imaginary Jake her prepared questions, with different appealing looks or poses.

As the time for departure approached, Violet advised Rose to wrap up warm. It was certainly going to be a very cold excursion!

Isaac and Jake waited patiently at the back door while Violet, irritated by Rose's tardiness, chivvied her to get a move on as she fiddled with the bow on her bonnet. "For goodness sake, Rose, the weather will whip that about anyway as soon as we get outside. Come on!! They're waiting for us!!!" Rose, muttering under her breath, still insisting on the last touch of perfection, on what was realistically a shoddy hat. Finally, down the stairs, all four wrapped up as best as they could, set out into the winter scene.

Joviality kept them warm as they strode out with excitement towards the lake. Truth be told, it was not really a lake at all but had become referred to as one over the years. The low lying fields around Broadway's neighbouring village Saintbury, regularly flooded following heavy rains. In the spring and autumn particularly, after lengthy periods of moisture had torrented down the hillside with nowhere to drain, the saturated ground pooled. Consequently, as the winter temperature dropped, it metamorphosed into a frozen arena of shallow ice, perfect for skating.

Once the group had turned the corner of the drive leading away from Bancroft House, the breeze was behind them and they were on the pathway towards the village, joining in with the throng of people all heading in the same direction. A shortcut across the frosty fields and the animated joviality of the atmosphere made the walk not seem so far and joyfully full of anticipation. A few couples passed the group of four, carrying skates. Violet watched them go by with envy, wishing she could be one of them ... yet reflecting ironically that she barely had a half decent pair of shoes!

The skating event had, over recent years, become a local tradition at this time of year and just about everybody in the village wanted to go. The sporting event was, however, becoming more than just about skating. It was a meeting place for friends, families or even a place to go to meet a beau or a sweetheart. Half a dozen little stalls had popped up here and there around the near side of the lake, selling warming spicy mulled wine – some also sold negus, the non-alcoholic version for the children and others sold queen drop biscuits and gingerbread.

It was simply exhilarating! The four companions approached the bustling hub of activity and found themselves a place by the lake where they felt it would be the best vantage point for seeing the skaters whizzing past, once the competitions began. Violet was jumping up and down on the spot, as much from excitement as from fending off the cold. Rose frantically rubbed her gloved hands together and periodically put them to her mouth to blow hot breath onto them in an attempt to keep warm. The hot breath vapour was visible in the still and icy late afternoon air around everybody's mouth as they chatted animatedly about the scene. As it became dark, lanterns were lit and the scene became truly magical.

The young men agreed to leave Rose and Violet in their chosen place, while they went off to acquire some hot mulled wine. Rose and Violet watched the skaters preparing to race and enjoying the hubbub of activity. Eventually, some time later,

Isaac and Jake returned clutching four super sized tankards of mulled wine. "Oh my life!" Violet exclaimed! I can't possibly drink all of that!!" but nevertheless began to sip the warm liquid and loved the feel of its spices warming her inside. Rose, on the other hand took hers without hesitation and began to drink with gusto.

As the boys were distributing the steaming hot drinks to the girls, the gun shot rang out to mark the first of the races. With a roar, instantly, everyone's focus was towards the lake and with a frisson of energy, screeches and cheers rang out across the stillness as onlookers cheered for whoever they wished to encourage. Laughter and joviality was so contagious, it spread like an effervescent wave along the lakeside, engulfing all spectators. Violet inched towards Jake. Just standing so close, brought her a sort of tingling joy. They found themselves randomly choosing the same competitor to win and whooped with jubilation when they won – or commiserated between themselves when they did not.

Violet had to admit that the mulled wine had certainly warmed her up! In fact she felt rather giddy and giggly – and liked it! Having said that, she was a sensible enough girl to know that any more of the amber liquid would not sit well with her, so she offered the remainder of the tankard to Jake. Before it could reach Jake's hand, however, Rose had snapped it up with relish and chided Violet for her feebleness. Violet raised an eyebrow but ignoring the jibe, thinking how immature Rose could sometimes be and turned towards the lake to realize there was to be a lull in the proceedings as the race participants took a break before the final set of races.

The anticipation was palpable now and things were getting really tense as the crowds sought to speculate and predict the winning team. Some friction started up around a bulk of men as they wagered on the winners. During the break, the four companions walked up to another of the mulled wine stands and considered a biscuit along with a drink. Violet refrained from another mulled wine but bought a small tankard of non-alcoholic negus as preference, together with a gingerbread. Rose had a further large mulled wine, as did Jake and Isaac.

Refreshments in hand, they turned to walk back to find roughly where they had been standing. Rose got caught behind another group of people and chanced to notice another goblet of hot mulled wine on the side of the stand, apparently belonging to nobody at all. Without hesitation and unobserved by the others, she surreptitiously snatched the pot and swigged back the alcoholic drink. Its strength taking her by surprise, made her splutter, but a second series of gulps saw the pot emptied. As though nothing had happened, she then followed the sight of Violet's dark green coat and moments later caught up with everyone, already absorbed in the start of the penultimate race.

By the time the final race had begun, the weather had really closed in and it was quite difficult to see the race contenders. As they reached the finish line, the result was difficult to call from a distance and a rumpus flared up, further along the lake's frozen edge between those who had wagered their coins. Spiked with curiosity, a surge of spectators pushed closer to see what was going on and in doing so, swept up Violet and Isaac, separating them from Jake and Rose.

Confused now, fumbling her way as close as she could to Jake's side, Rose felt rather hazy. It was as though she observed what was before her through a distant, moving fog and even her hearing seemed fuzzy. Whenever she spoke, it was as though it was not her own voice speaking and her mouth did not move as she wished... Surrounded by so much frenzy as spectators focused on the increasing tousle, the crowd pushed forward, jostling Rose as she continued to try to slurp at the last of her drink, spilling some as she went.

It seemed they were all heading back now towards the village and a swathe of people, all in unison moved forward past what had now become a fight and Rose was swept along with them as though in a dream. Jake seemed to be leading her along the pathway until eventually they found themselves in a clearing and he was saying something to her as though from a distance, yet his face was close in front of her. He didn't seem pleased... She tried to concentrate on her legs moving...

Chapter 10

From her deep sleep, Louise gave a sudden gasp. In one swift movement, she sat bolt upright. Her eyes shot wide open trying to make sense of the pitch-black darkness.... Her body still...paralysed. Her lungs were unable to breathe, as if compensating for her heightened sense of hearing. It was as though any miniscule body movement, any flinch, was audible to the blackness around her.

A doubt... what woke her? A dream? Imagination? Her mind replayed the subconscious moment. No...a noise! To her left... Nonsensically, she dared not even turn her head in the direction of the sound. Hot, trembling, her only solace was the whirr of words she spoke to herself deep inside her conscious mind – quiet, whispering words to comfort herself. Calm. Logic.

She was suddenly aware of her heart racing, thudding, bouncing inside her ribcage. Her throat pulsed. Slowly, slowly, without a single flicker of muscle movement, her peripheral vision sensed the outline of a shadowy image. It stood beside her. Immobile. Soundless ... but NOT her imagination! ....

With one swift movement, the shape lunged at her. Huge hands grasped her around her neck. Stinking, hot breath forced its way into her ear. Words threatened her with malice she cared not to ignore. Her body could not have screamed anyway, even if she commanded it...

The force pulled her carelessly from her mattress.

Momentarily she struggled against it but knew it was futile. Her small frame was inconsequential against his hulk. He was all the same annoyed at her fleeting resistance and tightened his grip with a muffled curse. With an easy movement he had hauled her up and across his shoulders and she hung like a piece of raw meat. Surfacing from her fear and confusion, she rallied against his strength and intuitively used her dangling legs to kick him as hard as she could. Her angry hands clawed at his greasy knotted hair to pull back his head and finding her voice, instinctively screamed in his ear with as much velocity as she could muster. The feisty onslaught took him aback and simultaneously finding himself at the top of the stairs with little light other than a slight cast of the moon from another room, he lost his footing. Obscenities flew from his sour breath as the pair plummeted downwards headfirst, crashing against the wood panelled wall and simultaneously snapping the wooden spindles on the opposite edge of the stairs until they landed with a final splat on the tiled hallway floor. A moment's silence and stillness ensued. Gaining a second breath, eyes stretched wide open, she waited for his fury.... but to her astonishment, he didn't move. Lifting her head and trying to slide her arm from beneath his heavy weight, she felt something wet on the floor beneath his head. He must be bleeding...

Still immobile, and seizing the opportunity, she carefully released herself from his jumbled body as though trying not to disturb a child from slumber, then quickly scrambled away on her hands and knees. Picking her way through the half dark, she found her feet and navigated the familiar space towards the internal door. Where the hell was everybody??? Surely that rumpus must have woken the whole household?? So where were they? She called out by name for each of her staff... There was nothing. Silence. It was as though she was entirely alone in the house, which terrified her. Her mind was scrambling thoughts -

not only was she scared just for her own safety but her concern was also for the staff in her employ. She found herself praying that they were safe and had not come to harm.

She was fairly sure her attacker was still motionless behind her. Nevertheless, she tried to move silently and cautiously for fear of arousing him from his unconsciousness. Catching the protruding leg of the sideboard with her toe, she again fell to the floor with a grimace, muttering inaudible words. She prayed the clatter had not awoken him and thus she continued her flight. Holding her breath she crawled along the floor, feeling her way towards the door into the passageway. Once there, she clawed herself up the oak panels until she could reach the door knob. Then gently and slowly, she turned the cold metal hand piece, grimacing as it creaked open towards her. Noiselessly, she manoeuvred herself around the heavy door and squeezed through the gap.

A little safer now, she scrambled onto her feet and hurriedly propelled herself forwards along the cold tiled passageway towards the kitchen. The embers of the fire were still enough to cast a glow into the corridor as well as around the room. Being able to see rather better, gave her some comfort and confidence. Completely upright now, Louise quickly grabbed a taper from the side table and shared a flame from the remnants of heat in the hearth. Grasping the flickering torch, she tiptoed further along the passageway towards Elders' office. No sign of anyone.

More frightened now, she turned towards the servants' stairwell intending to ascend. At that moment, she heard a muffled, grunting sound. Freezing once more, her body on full alert sensing her surroundings. The noise came again. Shaking, she glided in a surreal movement towards the sound which emanated from the under stairs cupboard. She hesitated but dared to stammer a whisper. "Who..... who's there???" The reply came with relief - another grunting sound but somehow she recognized the muffled sounds... "ELDERS!!!!!"

Without hesitation, she yanked at the small doorway. The weight of his released body flung Louise tumbling backwards with her manservant landing irreverently onto her legs. The candle spluttered as it fell to the floor but fortunately did not extinguish itself. Stifling a screech of shocked discomfort, she realized he was bound and gagged, his eyes glinting with shocked anger in the partial light. Leaning forward, pushing against his body weight, she hurriedly untied the gag from his mouth and they spoke simultaneously... "Are you alright?" "Yes, yes, of course...I'm fine," responded Elders indignantly in his usual dismissive way, as though being tied up in a cupboard was a regular occurrence. Retrieving the candle once more whilst Elders unravelled the rope from his wrists, "I'm not sure how long we are safe for though" warned Louise. "He's at the foot of the stairs, injured" she explained, assuming Elders knew to whom she was referring..."But I don't know if he comes to, how injured he is and if he can move. Quickly, we can't stay here!" she urged. "Where is everyone else?" she asked, her thoughts tumbling from her mind as she rubbed a swelling on the back of her head which she had suddenly become aware of. Elders detected slight panic in her voice.

Grovelling on the cold floor, still partially laying across Louise's legs, Elders was trying to untie his feet from the rope. "They're all out" Elders reminded his Ladyship impatiently. "It's the skating competition tonight by the lake – remember!!?" Louise quickly chided herself for forgetting the arrangement. "Oh, of course!! They'll be back late". That made Louise feel instantly better knowing that they must be safe but it did make her wonder if this intruder had realized she would be easy pickings with her staff being absent. A sick feeling crept over her wondering if whoever was behind this, had known her movements!

Just then, the back door was kicked open with a crash and a whoosh of white, freezing air blasted through threatening to extinguish her taper. Both Elders and Louise jumped and snapped up their heads towards the intrusion. Louise felt her heart could take no more shocks as it again thumped into heavy, heart-throbbing, irregular rhythm.

Battling through a sheet of blizzardous snow, which seemed to engulf him, Jake struggled through the narrow aperture of the doorway lugging a limp, awkward bundle... It took moments to realize... it was Rose!!!

It was hard to know who was the more taken aback. Louise and Elders looked upon the scene with incredulity – Rose was in a state of collapse and her small frame had clearly become a dead weight against Jake's meager frame. She was slipping from his clutches and about to slip from his hold. Where on earth had he carried her from?

Jake's brain, however, also tried to comprehend the scene in front of him, and he temporarily questioned his own degree of drunkenness! Was this really his mistress and the butler before him, apparently cavorting around on the floor in virtual blackness??? Jake was visibly relieved to allow Rose to slip from his arms onto the nearest chair with a grunt of exhaustion.

"Whatever's happened Jake?" snapped Louise then tutted her indifference to the answer. "Never mind that for now – we are in trouble here Jake – we can't stay here, we are all in danger!"

Jake looked even more confused! "I don't understand Ma'am. See, Rose, she had too much mulled wine and she kept falling over see... so I thought I'd best get her home like but then her legs seemed not to work well and so I..."

"Jake... yes that's very thoughtful of you but... **somebody is in the house!**" she hissed in order to emphasise her words. "I think he's injured but..." Her voice trailed off... Suddenly, for the first time.

Slowly registering what his mistress was saying, Jake's forehead furrowed with concern. "Are you hurt, Ma'am??"

At that moment, Rose groaned, then giggled... Her slumped body slid uncontrollably in slow motion from the chair to the floor with a heavy thud and Elders lunged forward quickly to save her head from crashing to the floor. Unfortunately, with that, she vomited directly into his lap.

Chapter 11

Clearly, the intruder was strong and burly. So, after some rapidly whispered consideration, they decided safety was in numbers if they were to overcome him and safely apprehend him. It seemed prudent to put Rose on the rug in the corner of the kitchen, safely aside out of the way should the intruder come to life!!! Elders would manage that. Jake went out to warn the returning party of the situation.

With guilt, Louise suddenly thought of Betsy! Oh my God what about Betsy?!! Please God she was safe, she prayed! She stealthily ran upstairs with her taper and quietly turned the door knob to the maid's room, heart racing half expecting the woman to be bound and gagged but with enormous relief, rather she found her snoring soundly in her bed.

'Betsy!' she whispered loudly. No movement... "Betsy!!" she tried even louder. Louise reached out and vigorously shook the body beneath the blankets and Betsy screamed herself awake, almost falling out of bed with shock. "Nation!!!!" She shouted without being fully awake. Her sleeping bonnet pulled askew across part of one eye and drool running across her cheek. Louise rattled her body further to shock her maid into the moment. Then with a forefinger to her mouth, Louise, silenced her maid urgently.

Once compos mentis, if a little confused, Betsy returned downstairs with Louise just as Jake, Violet and Isaac were returning. The latecomers had a thousand questions about all that had passed since they were separated at the lake but instead they faced an unexpectedly sobering welcome home! Violet and Isaac had been under strict instruction from Jake to tread stealthily back into the house where they met with Elders and Louise at the back door, now armed with fire irons: the best impromptu weapons they could muster.

Ever resourceful, Violet took it upon herself to gather a few candles and light them, distributing them to whoever had a free hand. The quickly hatched plan was to return to 'the body' dead or alive 'en masse'. Together, hushed, they moved back along the passageway towards the panelled door, still ajar from Louise's exit. The tension between the group was palpable and Betsy thought she might actually pass out with fear. Carefully, one by one, sliding through the partially open doorway, they crept along the hallway towards the foot of the stairs...

Squinting downwards Louise gasped in disbelief... there was no dead body, as she suspected there might be. Partly in gracious thanks she had not been party to a death, she gave a sigh of something close to relief but this was quickly followed, by a stirring of panic through her veins. "He's gone!!!"... she whispered...

In comical disbelief, they all stared at the empty, candlelit spot at the base of the stairs, then looked at each other, then looked to Louise as though searching for answers. "He's gone!!!" she gasped again, as though to confirm he WAS there and she was NOT going mad!!! Rose held a candle closer to the spot where Louise said she had left him. A pool of sticky redness remained. "See!!" croaked Louise as though this offered proof at least that she was not going crazy with imagination.

Elders grabbed Jake by the arm and instructed him to go to the Library off the hall and the salon next to it to check if there were any signs of him... Isaac was dispatched in the opposite direction to the morning room and dining room. Elders then insisted Louise to stay put with Violet and Betsy and urged her to scream for dear life should he return upon her... He himself would head towards the front parlour to investigate.... Those windows lead directly onto the garden.

Left in the almost dark with the diminished light of fewer candles, suddenly, Louise felt exhausted and vulnerable with a chill running through her bones. She shook herself. Her duty was to look after her staff who were by now visibly shaking with fear.

Each of the scouts returned one by one with no sighting of the culprit.

For a split moment, Louise thought she was truly in a dream. Had she really imagined all of this? "Don't be ridiculous!" she chided herself. Her bruised body from the fall was enough to prove to her that it happened – unless she had been having a nightmare?? She only had to glance at the bloodied floor to know this was very real! Perplexed, they silently made their way back to the kitchen.

Without conscious thought, Betsy heated up some milk. Louise flopped into the old armchair next to the near dead fire and Elders, seeing his Ladyship shivering from shock, reached for a rug from the store and suggested Louise wrap it around her shoulders. He began to stoke the embers in the hope it would relight itself. Louise suggested to Jake that he and Isaac lift Rose upstairs to the bed chamber. Violet should accompany them for propriety's sake and help her into bed. All three, turning towards Rose in the corner of the room where they had left her, chorused in unison – "Where's Rose gone?!" ....

His temper was as filthy as his breath when he came to at the foot of the stairs. The little witch had got the better of him and escaped! His head bleeding and banging sore, he squinted open his eyes and found his bearings in the darkness, confused as to which way he came in. Dragging himself half upright to get his balance again, he staggered towards a doorway. He could hear hushed voices from somewhere... Instinctively he turned to head in the opposite direction.

Trying a doorknob, he made his way through a room towards another door. He stopped dead. Someone was coming in. He dropped with a thud to his knees behind a chair and lay still, hoping the sound was muted enough not to give away his presence. Sensing movement around the room and the flicker of a flame, he held his breath. The steps drew closer and irrationally he closed his eyes. After little time, the hurried footsteps receded and were gone. He breathed again.

Another moment to recover before he struggled off his knees and continued his search for an exit. Heading across a narrow passageway and towards the light of a dying fire, everything was quiet here until he saw something move on the floor. Thinking it was a dog, he again stopped statue still in the dread of being rumbled. As he focused though, he realized it to be a woman.

Still feeling the fury of failure in not capturing his intended prey, he thought to remove this God given compensation lying before him on the floor. Easy prey this time!! That would appease his boss for sure!! He grinned as he swept down to drag the girl up off the floor and hung her in his familiar way over his shoulder. She protested incoherently and vomited again ... Almost blasphemous language emitted from his mouth but he just needed to get out without more ado and get the hell out of there. What a stinking night this was turning out to be in more ways than one!

God this was hard!! Carrying a dead weight through swirling snow and freezing cold. His own head was really sore. At least this one was not fighting like they usually do...

There was no way he was going to make it back to base without kipping overnight. It was just too much. It had all gone so wrong tonight but at least he wasn't going back empty handed. He might not have got the one he was sent out to abduct but this wench would be good for bargaining with, so he'd better make sure she didn't slip through his fingers like the last one or else he'd be in for a beating.

Since she was half collapsed anyway, he decided to stop off at the Coach House – and at least enjoy some ale – he deserved at least that!! Trouble is, if she woke up enough, she might get awkward and cause a scene. Best use the Godfrey's Cordial he brought with him for emergencies. That would shut her up for a while. He stopped some way before the Coach House and dropped the girl heavily on the snow-covered ground. She groaned as much from the shock of the fall as the pain she suffered in her head. She tried to scramble to her feet but he caught her round her throat and delighted in telling her in grotesque detail where she was bound for. She could barely take in the threat of the workhouse and continued her struggle to flea.

He rattled around his pockets until he found the small tin bottle of laudanum mixture and freed the stopper. Without ceremony, he grabbed the hair at the back of her head and yanked her skull backwards, thrusting her chin upwards and expertly poured the content down her throat. She gagged at the intrusive syrup and spluttered but enough of it was swallowed and after a few moments, she once again became limp and compliant. Hauling her up again, it was still some way to trudge with this increasingly heavy burden. His head was bleeding more now, running down the back of his neck.

Chapter 12

Tobias lifted a sleepy little girl from his carriage into the now blizzardous conditions. The weather had indeed continued to worsen and Tobias was grateful for his driver's sensible counsel to pull in at the coach house tucked into the hillside part way up Fish Hill. It would have been most foolish to continue.

They were not, however, the only travellers to conclude the same but despite the hostelry being busy, Tobias was fortunate enough to secure a clean room upstairs with a fire where they could stay overnight. He arranged for the driver to stable the horses and insisted he sleep alongside them overnight to ensure they were not stolen.

Tobias made sure Izzy had had a hearty meal then settled her in the cot alongside his bed. Once she was asleep, he went back downstairs for a hot whisky before he too retired. His mind was still whirring from the day's events and believed sleep was some way off for him.

He had not long secured his chair by the fire and opened up his book, when the door flew open bringing with it a flurry of snow and an icy blast of freezing air, which frenzied the flames in the grate. Had that not been enough to draw his attention, the unpalatable stench, which followed, did!

Tobias looked up to see a burly, unkempt male entered, half carrying and half dragging a young woman who appeared to be somewhat drunk. Her clothes wet as though she'd fallen over in the snow. There was a stink of vomit and the girl seemed to be struggling against him. He kept a grip of her as he demanded a jar of ale, then carelessly threw the girl into a chair and grumbling, massaged his cramped shoulder with relief from her weight. It was then that Tobias noticed blood on the back of his head, matted into his greasy hair.

Intrigued by all this, Tobias again turned his attention to the girl who was now trying to get up from the chair but her legs were unsteady making it easy for him to yank her back into the seat, swearing as he did so. More curious, Tobias continued to observe with discretion this wild looking unlikely couple, until the girl lifted her head and wiped away a curtain of hair from her face. It looked very much like she was trying to fight against him but his huge hands were easily quelling her struggle. In that moment, recognition stabbed at Tobias. His heart thumped with concern. He could be mistaken and looked again. No mistake, this young woman was indeed Louise's maid!!! What the hell was she doing here and in this state? She was certainly being held against her will.

Now what?? The man was such a hulk that if provoked could easily take down Tobias and looked very much as though he had already done so that very night. How could he possibly get Rose away from him without a feisty confrontation? He watched as the bedraggled man gulped down the ale in front of him and wiping his mouth with the back of his bloodied hand, shouted another ale be brought to him.

The Innkeeper, reaping the benefit of the bad weather, was taken by surprise with the number of customers and needed to go to the back room to get more ale, almost visibly rubbing his hands with delight at the thought of more profit!

Next to the warmth of the fire, it seemed that Rose had fallen asleep, her head fallen back against the chair and mouth open, drooling. The room had become much quieter now as guests headed to their rooms and it gave Tobias an idea, so he took his opportunity.

Firstly, he took it into his own hands to stoke the fire good and hot. Warmth and alcohol would be his best friend in this situation. Making as though he was heading towards the bar. He then paused and hovered casually by the repulsive fellow, himself already soporific from the warmth of the room after the cold outside and the night's events. "It's a fair terrible night out there!" Tobias opened up a friendly dialogue. Nodding towards the girl he continued, "Your companion looks like she's not great company! Mind if I join you? – I hate drinking alone!"

Before the man could engage his brain to respond, the Innkeeper returned with a cask and Tobias beckoned him to bring a jug of whisky along with the ale and with temerity, sat alongside the stinking couple. "Not going to get much joy out of her tonight then my friend" Tobias half laughed then continued, " Looks like she's had a stomach full already! – Bet you're a good drinker eh? – you like your ale? – I prefer the harder stuff! Want some?"

Again, he didn't wait for a reply but grabbed another glass from the bar and poured two generous short drinks, pushing the first towards the hulk of a man who responded with a single grunt and snatched the drink swigging it back immediately without considering the presumption of this unfamiliar man. Slamming the glass back on the table, he then continued with his ale while Tobias poured another whisky in his tumbler. Tobias fiddled with his own cup pretending to savour the flavour and rambled on with a dialogue, which did not require any answers, periodically topping up the stranger's glass as he continued to accept the generosity of the philanthropic coach house guest, without question.

Finally, Tobias, full of apparent 'hail fellow, well met', made to go to bed, leaving the odd couple alone in the corner of the room propped up and incoherent. The room had thankfully become empty now. Tobias stood making inane conversation with the innkeeper for long enough to be sure that the man in the corner had completely fallen asleep.

His next task was to distract the Innkeeper for some considerable moments. Offering him a generous tip, he asked for him to take a message to his driver out in the stable. The grateful owner accepted the sweetener and as hoped, left immediately through the back door and into the freezing night air. Acting quickly now, Tobias moved towards Rose and with as much dexterity as he could muster, struggled to lift her graceless, lifeless form, sliding her slowly with trepidation, away from the suspicious man. She groaned slightly causing him to freeze momentarily in fear of enraging the bear of a figure beside her but as her head wobbled forward again into silence, he then managed to sweep her up into his arms and with a deep breath turned to take her upstairs. Still holding his breath, he finally reached the top of the steep stairs and fumbled to open the bedroom door.

Thankfully, Izzy was blissfully asleep in the cot bed nearest to the fire. Tobias made his way in the glow of light from the dying embers and headed straight for the poster bed, laying Rose heavily on the counterpane. He stood upright, stretching his back with a silent groan and breathed with relief. She immediately rolled over into a comfortable position, took a deep sigh and continued to sleep heavily.

Turning now to secure the door, Tobias looked around the room and seeing an uninviting chair, flopped into it. Without a second's pause, he fell into an uncomfortable asleep.

Chapter 13

No sleep that night for Louise.

Wide awake now with adrenalin, her mind in turmoil. She was beginning to feel nauseous with shock and her headache had not abated but rather worsened. Betsy made a jug of hot milk and best brandy for her Ladyship and Elders, who was also looking rather grey.

It seems that Elders was taken by complete surprise with a firm hand sweeping round him from behind and without ability to shout out, he was bundled to the floor and bound up with a ripped rag tied around his mouth and manoeuvered into the cupboard. He had had no chance to see the attacker but he too commented on his stench. Between Elders and Louise they were certain their attacker had been one and the same person – no accomplice.

Rose had gone!! In a heartbeat, Isaac raced up the stairs. He was certain Rose, having evidently vomited again, would have made her way up to bed whilst they were searching for the intruder. Shocked that she wasn't there, he continued to check all the other rooms, calling out her name as he went, his heart banging with panic. Grabbing a lantern from the back door, he returned to the kitchen he yelled at Jake to come and search outside with him – he had no idea why she would have gone outside but if she wasn't inside....

The snow was falling heavily now. It had settled deeply on the ground. It was difficult to see any signs of tracks but since the snow was falling fast that was not too much of a surprise. Hopelessly, they returned inside and sat up together in the kitchen worrying and trying to fathom where she could be and if the intruder had abducted her – and why? Elders tried to insist Louise got back to bed but she would hear nothing of it. How could she possibly rest while Rose was missing? Together they made a plan and as soon as daylight broke, the boys went out again to look for Rose.

In the morning light, Louise and Elders returned to where she had left the intruder and could see that there were traces of dripped blood where he had moved off towards the garden room, which lead on to the kitchen. How stupid had they been! He must have taken this route towards the back door to escape while they came through the house the other way. Opportunistically, he came across Rose and took her in place of Louise. But why?? Why ever did he want either of them? Louise wished now she hadn't fought him off. If he had taken her, then Rose would now be safe! No matter how much Elders tried to reason with her, Louise continued to punish herself for the loss of Rose who was placed here in her care. Elders felt sure the boys would return carrying her in with nothing more than a chill but Louise's instinct was less hopeful.

Isaac and Jake worked well as a team, starting their search with the outbuildings and the near fields, then on towards the village. Asking around and knocking on doors but nobody had heard or seen anything unusual. There were no strangers in the area that anyone could recall. Freezing cold now, soaked through after trudging through the deep and drifted snow they returned unrewarded and exhausted back to Bancroft House.

The disappointment crushed Louise. How could this be happening?

She then had a terrible thought! They would have to tell Rose's father that his daughter had gone missing – likely abducted. She really feared facing his wrath and dreaded his venomous reaction. However, the weather was certainly closing in and it would be madness to venture out now to the far side of the village to try to find him, which gave Louise legitimate reason for not doing so just yet and also gave them more time to make a plan to find her.

Rose had felt herself turn over on the floor rug where they had left her in her wine induced stupour...Trying to open her eyes, her blurred vision could make out something unfamiliar but it was swirling and fuzzy. Her head squelched and she felt ghastly. She tried to speak but her mouth would not form a single sound.

The unfamiliar shape moved towards her and hauled her onto her dainty feet, though her legs caved from under her and he gathered her up unceremoniously like a loose sack of flour.

She had no idea for how long she had been passed out but woke as she was propelled against the edge of a wall from behind and a hand – a stinking, rough hand, wrapped around her face stopping her breath. They were outside.... She was cold. It was snowing. She felt terrible. Her legs wouldn't work. He was lifting her. No dragging her...Where were they? He tugged open the door and whispered threats in her ear. Somehow she was dropped in a chair. The lights were fuzzy. She could make out a fire and people. It was quite noisy.

Trying to get back up again, a heavy hand pushed her back down again. "Where am I?" she muttered. Filthy breath told her to shut up and stay where she was otherwise he'd have to carry out the threat he'd already explained. Her vision simply would not work and her stomach still lurched. Her brain tried to scramble what he meant by the threat and she just couldn't quite grasp what he had said. Again oblivion overcame her. In and out of wooziness, she remembered a patchwork of moments. She knew she had been to the lake – how cold it was – snowing...

Oh God... she'd been drinking hadn't she – Is that why she felt so terrible? Nothing more would come to her.... Her feet were cold. So cold. A vague memory then passed through her mind. Unsure: "Had she been lying on the kitchen floor at Bancroft House.... in the kitchen?? What was she doing in the kitchen on the floor for goodness sake?" she wondered curiously...

It was so warm here in this place. She could smell vomit. Oh God, she did not feel good! She half opened her unwilling eyes. A fire. Yes there was a fire in front of her. Hot.... A man came to sit by her...Talking. Erm...yes, he was talking ... A gentle voice ... safe... Did she know him???

Blackness lifted. A little voice wakened her. Excited. A little girl? Jumping up and down with joy... who?... Such a pretty dress. Bancroft House – Izzy. The visitor... Rose turned her head towards the light and standing there was ...Mr. Woolmer. What??? She jumped up from her pillow. Her head spun and she collapsed back down again holding her head in both hands. "Rose...Rose... Listen to me" said the voice. "You're safe. It's alright."

The Innkeeper had found Tobias's driver and given the exact instruction to have his carriage ready for first light the next morning and the coach was to be driven round to the front of the coach house. No time for refreshments, Tobias had woken a bewildered Rose, confused to find herself in this irrational situation – in a strange room with Mr. Woolmer and Izzy. Izzy on the other hand was excited beyond words to find her new best friend sharing a room with her. Tobias, now worried for propriety, wondered how he had managed to get himself in this situation and feared for how he might extricate himself from it unscathed of reputation, for himself and for Rose!

As soon as Rose was conscious enough, Tobias hastily reassured her that she was safe with him and impressed upon her that they had to get her back to Bancroft House without ado. They were all possibly in danger if this did not go to plan. It was imperative to get out of the coach house as quickly and as unobserved as possible, hopefully without encountering her abductor, who, God willing would still be in an intoxicated stupour where Tobias had left him.

Izzy was enraptured by the whole adventure and silent secrecy and barely able to contain herself but knew she must listen to uncle Tobias's instructions to keep Rose safe. She wasn't quite sure why Rose would not be safe but sensed this was not the time for her to question what was going on. She was happy enough to see Rose again and be going back to see the nice Lady in the big house. Possibly, she could feed Purrcillus again! The thought of that in itself, distracted her from how her tummy rumbled with hunger.

With a plan of action, rapidly instructed by Tobias, they would hopefully escape into the carriage unnoticed. He would go first to pay for their lodgings and check the status of the obnoxious man. If once again, he could give the Innkeeper a task to distract him, he could, moments later, confirm with a signal to Rose that all was safe. The girls would stealthily descended the narrow, wooden stairs, cross the bar room and exit the door at the front of the coach house. As hoped, the man was still where Tobias had left him, slumped with intoxication and totally unaware of Rose's rescue. Also to plan, Tobias's coach was immediately in front of the exit, almost obliterated by a snowstorm.

The weather was by now treacherous and Tobias's driver was not at all happy to be risking the short journey back down the hill. Tobias impressed upon him the necessity to return to Bancroft House as a matter of great urgency, otherwise the young woman could be in possible danger. He offered a significant 'tip' and pleaded the 'errand of mercy' so well, that the driver rose to the challenge and set off precariously back down the steep hill.

Chapter 14

After the initial panic of realizing Rose had gone, Isaac begged Elders to bring in the Peelers. The butler asked him to refrain from using the vernacular but said that as soon as it was daylight he would of course send for the Police. Hearing this, Jake, froze to the spot with guilt. His imagination ran riot, fearing that somehow they would sense his criminal act and his dealings with the man at the house would be uncovered. He was a terrible liar and felt that somehow it was bound to come about that he had buried a dead body!

Isaac persisted. "But Sir, me and Betsy was talking yesterday, Sir. We've heard there's someone gone missing – a man. They say he's supposed to be a detective Sir. Seems he was onto something here in the village but now he can't be found." Elders scoffed, "Well I can't see how that could possibly be connected to Rose going missing, Isaac!"

"No, but they tried to take Her Ladyship first though Sir, didn't they?" Isaac countered. Realising Isaac had a point, Elders looked concerned and looked to Louise for permission to call the Police. Jake could swear his heart actually stopped. There seemed to be an interminable pause while Louise considered the suggestion before she replied.

Unwittingly, Jake exhaled loudly with relief, when Louise said she preferred to wait until a further search of the grounds had been completed, before they rushed into calling for outside assistance. Jake made a mock yawn and stretched his arms above his head as though exhausted, in the hope of disguising his sound of reprieve. Louise continued completely unaware of his theatrical performance, convincing Elders that she didn't want word to get back to Rose's father, before she had had chance to tell him herself. Besides, she would rather not look like an over-reacting female fool, if Rose was then to be found in an outhouse. Should it be that Rose had not appeared by mid morning, then yes, the Police were to be involved. Jake relapsed into fear.

Betsy and Violet had tried to continue with routine tasks, just to keep to some normality to the strange morning but also as Betsy said, the chores wouldn't do themselves! Violet made some bread and Betsy some of Louise's favourite cake in the hope that the smell would entice her to eat something. It didn't! Isaac checked in on the horses and couldn't help himself from checking the barns and outhouses again, even though this had all been done a short time before. He couldn't believe Rose could simply have disappeared from under their noses. Jake stoked up the fires and brought in more wood. They were going to need plenty if this snowstorm was going to last. He made sure the chickens were fed and kept safe in the barn. Distracted and worried, he took time to refresh their straw.

Louise, paced up and down constantly, ignoring the pleas of Betsy to 'not take on so'. She went over and over the events of the previous evening and with Elders' patient listening, she became more convinced that whoever it was that tried to take her, had instead taken Rose. What she could not fathom, was why? Who would want to abduct her? Where would they take Rose – and worse, what would they do with her?? She felt sick.

Elders saw the carriage arrive at Bancroft House and without the necessity for Tobias ringing the bell, Elders had quizzically opened the door in anticipation. With relief, he then saw Rose and with unusual urgency, called for his Ladyship to come quickly to the hall.

Louise's face was one of stunned relief. A thousand questions ran through her mind... but first to get the young girl back in the house and into Betsy's motherly care. She called upon Violet to attend to Izzy, with an unspoken communication to keep her occupied and charged Isaac with making sure the driver was made comfortable in the kitchen and the horses were accommodated. Louise then escorted Tobias into the warmth of the parlour. Without request, Elders brought a tray of hot drinks for them both and thought to put a plate of Betsy's morning baking onto a plate to coax Louise with some food at least. Had Louise not been made of stronger stuff, she would by now have resorted to tears, if only from relief! Her ordeal last night in itself would have had most young women take to their bed for a week but in addition, she had been so very worried and frightened for Rose. The sheer comfort of having her home was indescribable but Louise's greatest reaction had been the unexpected sight of Tobias again. She wanted to greet him like an old friend and welcome him 'home'. The strangest feeling.

They sat for some time either side of the blazing fire, updating each other on the bizarre events which had once again brought them together and as much as Louise was horrified to hear about Rose's abduction, Tobias was visibly outraged at Louise's terrifying experience. He watched her, transfixed, as she described her fear and desperately wanted to reach forward and comfort her – if only he could, just for a moment, hold her.

Louise confided in him about Elders' evident concern regarding Isaac's rumour, of a missing detective. She did so, hoping he would help her to dismiss any link. In a bid to comfort her, Tobias gave her the reassurances she clearly craved, however he was not so ready to do so for himself. It seemed tenuous but it was rather a coincidence that a missing person followed by an attempted abduction then a kidnap in the same small country village, were not linked. He owed it to Lord Dorchester to make sure his daughter was safe before he left her home.

It was difficult to find the words for Louise to thank Tobias but he did not need any. His own reward was being in the right place at the right time and being able to bring Rose back to safety. He dismissed the thoughts that there was another bonus in achieving his rescue mission and returning to Bancroft House but he must not think on that now.

It didn't ever seem to reach daylight all day. The tapers were constantly lit around the rooms and by mid afternoon, Betsy suggested closing the curtains to preserve the interior heat. Jake seemed to have a continuous round of keeping the fires roaring and later in the evening he prepared the hot charcoal for the bed warmers. Darting about the house was a good excuse for him to eavesdrop. He needed to keep aware of what was going to be done about involving the police. Please God they did not need to involve them now that Rose was home.

Once Rose was warm and fed, Louise sent for her to go to the drawing room. She and Tobias needed to get as much information out of her about her abduction. Rose trembled at the thought of being called to her Ladyship. Her childhood fears of being beaten had still not left her, nor perhaps ever would. She also knew deep down that this meant she would lose her job. Perhaps it was reaction setting in now from the terrifying events of last night but she suddenly plummeted in spirit and began to cry. Heartily cry! How could she go back to her father and tell him she got drunk and then abducted. He would be fearfully angry and she would undoubtedly get the worst of all beatings. Her legs could hardly support her as she stood up from the fireside chair, sobbing like never before. Betsy brusquely told her to pull herself together as nobody liked a sniveler but then feeling a pang of remorse at her own sharpness, tutted as only Betsy could and dug into her apron pocket to give the young girl a handkerchief. With encouragement, she told her gently to take a deep breath, straighten her back and push up her chin. As Betsy watched her bravely go up the stairs, it surprised her that she actually felt sorry for the girl, reminding herself she was still really nothing much more than a child.

With immense relief that she was not in trouble, Rose made profuse apologies for all that had happened. She babbled through more tears as she spoke to Mr. Woolmer, thanking him for all his kindness in rescuing her and bringing her home. The phrase touched Louise: Rose considered this as her home! Tobias too, accepted her clumsy thanks, seeing in Rose an older version of Izzy, vulnerable and innocent.

Rose's account of her abduction was not always coherent but with prompting, she was able to describe the repulsive man who took her and how he had smelt vile and thrown her over his shoulder to get her out of the house and into the cold. Louise, engulfed in her description, silently put her hand to her face and briefly closed her eyes, cringing with disgust to remember her own hideous experience, which mirrored that of Rose's. Her fleeting reaction was not lost on Tobias who recognised something akin to admiration or even pride for the way in which she stoically dealt with such a horrendous experience. Finding himself absorbed in her feminine elegance as though time stood still, it took him moments before he could bring himself back to concentrate on Rose's encounter.

Rose continued, telling the now attentive couple of his threats to take her to the workhouse and what she would become there and how his boss would pay him a handsome reward for getting her there. She cried again to remember how frightened she was through that awful fog of alcohol and felt very stupid.

Hearing the word 'workhouse', Tobias could not contain his anger. He paced the room, infuriated by what he had heard, and vowed to find this man and his boss who was obviously orchestrating bringing in waifs and strays to augment his workforce. His mind instantly flashed back to the abysmal conditions in which he found Izzy in that workhouse and his heart raced with anger. It was imperative that he found out who was behind this scam, endangering the lives of these two young women and no doubt many others. This must stop!!

What they could not fathom, however, was why try to take Louise? She had only just come to the area and had no real connection with anyone. She knew of nobody who bore a grudge. Yet, as soon as that thought was registered, Louise considered the incident with Jake in the wood alongside her land. But that was absurd to connect it to an abduction!! It made no sense!! Tobias saw the thoughtful frown flash across her face and insisted on her explaining. Perhaps there was more to this incident than Louise was aware of? Tobias needed to speak directly with Jake. He would have to choose his moment.

Rose was given permission to rest up, given her unfortunate experience but she elected to return to work as soon as she was cleaned up. She was utterly embarrassed at the predicament she had found herself in and the worry she had caused her Ladyship after all Louise had done for her. The least she could do was to get on with work as she was paid to do. This, in itself, pleased Louise and impressed both Betsy and Elders who both then conceded that Louise's decision to take her on, had not been totally in vain.

Heavy grey clouds continued to spill out their white flakes, which stuck to windows and built up against the doorways, obliterating pathways with no chance of safely hitching up the horses to Tobias's carriage. Louise did not seem overly concerned about the delay in Tobias and Izzy leaving the house – rather she seemed comfortable in the likelihood of them having to stay overnight. Of course this was simply because she could not possibly send them out into unsafe road conditions and because

Tobias had been brave enough to save Rose's life and bring her home. Irrationally, she also felt that after last night's fiasco, she would feel safer with Tobias close by.

Louise requested dinner be served early and accommodation be prepared for their unexpected guests. Violet had instruction to have Louise's father's room prepared for Mr. Woolmer, as this could quickly be redressed in time for her father's imminent arrival and Izzy would need to share the attic room with Rose, since they seemed to get along well, if Violet would share with Betsy for the night. Betsy was not altogether pleased at Violet's enforced encroachment of her space but since it was only for a night, simply sighed to herself impatiently.

Jake was to bring Mr. Woolmer's small travel bag upstairs and Tobias was waiting for him in the allocated master bedroom and ready to ask him some questions.

Chapter 15

The next morning saw even deeper snow. The coach and its passengers would be going nowhere today! Tobias made apologies to Louise for their further intrusion but it would seem that neither of them were genuinely inconvenienced or truly sorry to have their stay extended. Izzy was simply ecstatic. Louise's head was still sore as a bleak reminder of recent events and her morning conversations with Tobias were dominated by the topic of the abduction.

Tobias's dialogue with Jake left him feeling concerned. Having contrived to speak with him alone, Tobias quickly assessed that Jake seemed like a friendly, personable sort of young man who easily fell into polite chatter. Taking the first opportunity, Tobias conversationally brought about the subject of 'his recent incident near the wood'. Quite unexpectedly, he did not anticipate the boy's demeanour to dramatically change. He was clearly defensive and gave but the briefest of responses. Tobias asked how his Ladyship had reacted to the incident and was interested to learn that she had subsequently sent Jake to the neighbour's house with a letter. Jake was thereafter almost mute. He became so jittery and flustered as though he couldn't wait to leave the room and be gone. It wasn't difficult to suspect that he was hiding something.

Tobias preferred not to divulge his concerns to Louise. Importantly, he felt uncomfortable about not knowing the identity of the abductor and if he might return. Until it was known why Louise was the first target to be kidnapped, he would not know if she was still in danger. That fact alone unnerved him.

If the landowner next door, apparently a Mr. Partridge according to Jake, was bearing a grudge that was also a concern. He could not believe there was a link with the attempted kidnap, but it would be good to eliminate him from his worries. Somehow, he needed to find out more about Mr. Partridge.

He thanked fate for sending such inclement weather! He needed time to reassure himself that Louise would be in no further danger before he left. He wondered where Rose's abductor was now and reflected on Rose's comment that he had threatened her with the workhouse and spoke of a boss who would give him a sound beating if he failed to complete his task. Who was that? Tobias tasked himself to unravel whatever it was that lay behind the events of the last few weeks.

Unaware of any concerns Elders or Tobias now had about Jake's letter delivery to the neighbour's house, Louise had no reason to connect this with the intrusion the other night. Tobias casually asked Louise about her neighbours and she mentioned Isaac's warning about not getting involved in a dispute with Mr. Partridge. Louise passed it off as unimportant but triggering Tobias's concern further, he now needed a reason to do some investigating without frightening Louise.

However, Louise really had to pull herself together. Christmas was approaching... Louise used to love this time of year before her mamma passed away. It held such excitement and fun and romantic notions of love and courtship. Everything seemed happier and full of promise, knotted together with the nostalgia of childhood. Perhaps now that she was resident at Bancroft House, she could retrieve some of those happier feelings.

She recalled her memory images of December fields lying bare of crops yet yielding a wonderment of mother nature's artistry. The muted colours of silhouetted trees against grey skies and the baron fields sprinkled with freezing white. Sheep huddled against walls for shelter - their woolly coats seemed a contradiction; intended to keep them warm and protected against the cold, yet hanging uncomfortably heavy, in the dampness. Sometimes in the early afternoon sunshine, the bark of some trees appeared with a cast of bright green as though a promise of spring may be on the horizon – but, teasingly, there would still be some months to wait.

However, this year's weather was proving more brutal. The heaviness of the snowy blizzards had transformed the views, mutating the landscape into almost unrecognizable vistas. The darkness of solid cloud never seemed to lift from morning till night and the day had no distinction other than time itself. Despite recent events, inside the sturdy walls of Bancroft House, Louise felt cocooned and was determined to make the house into a festive home.

There was good reason this week to prepare for the most special of yuletide occasions. Just as she had arrived at Bancroft House, she had received a letter from distant family friends who would be travelling up from the south on their arduous coach journey to visit their relatives further north for the festive season. They had anticipated that Louise and her father would be in residence at Bancroft House at that time of year and hedged her bets on acquiring accommodation along their way. Louise had written directly back to them without ado, offering the unassuming hospitality of Bancroft House as a resting place to break their long and undoubtedly very cold journey.

Louise was anxious that she could provide a suitable welcome never having herself executed such an undertaking before. She had seen her mother orchestrate such hospitality many times before but had never taken on the responsibility herself and she was well aware that she had limited staff here to do so. However, she reasoned to herself that it would be a short stay over and they would surely not over expect of her, knowing her circumstances. The welcome created would be the best she could muster and decorating the rooms was to her a therapeutic joy and with or without guests, she loved to bring the festive cheer alive.

Louise reminisced over her memories of Aunt Fee. She was of course not an Aunt at all but an aged friend of a cousin of her mother's. She remembered that she suffered constantly with a most debilitating respiratory condition. She recalled the ageing woman from childhood and held an image of an overweight, somewhat humorless, hypochondriac, who travelled with an equally overweight gent whom she now presumed to be her husband, known to Louise as Uncle Gerald.

Recollecting this man, it was also a concern to Louise that Uncle Gerald's own health was deteriorating. His condition, however, was rather more self-inflicted. It had become apparent that he was inclined to over-imbibe of his favourite tipple and so often spent long hours indulging and a further many hours recovering before recommencing the whole procedure over again! In between times, his mobility was suffering and he could be something of a liability if not constantly under supervision.

That considered, it would be so wonderful to fill this beautiful home with guests whom she could revel in pandering to and fussing over. She could only assume that the weather would have drastically improved to allow their journey and of course, for the same reason, Tobias and Izzy would be gone. At this notion, her heart made a little plummet of realization. How strange – they would be gone! With a shrug of disregard, she continued with her planning.

With any degree of good fortune, her father would also have managed to join them by the time they were here, to help her host the party of virtual strangers. She would decorate the house like it had never been done before. It was becoming more fashionable now to bring in the outdoors and celebrate the beauty of the countryside during this festive season.

This time of year was becoming quite a romantic and magical time with candles on Christmas trees and wrapped gifts to exchange with loved ones. Family and friends visited each other and the mystical imagery of Father Christmas bringing gifts for children becoming a popular excitement for all ages. Louise was excited to embrace it all here at Bancroft House and couldn't wait to dress the house and welcome her guests in the best festive spirit.

Louise allocated herself a favourite little notebook, especially for the purpose of the upcoming visitor's stay. She needed it to be a huge personal success – mostly to prove to herself but also her dear papa, that she was capable as a hostess and that he could be proud of her. She began making notes of little details as they occurred to her so that she wouldn't forget any of her sudden inspirational ideas and added sketches to her notebook as she went. Louise loved to write and draw. She found it therapeutic and absorbing as well as entertaining and she could actually spend hours writing poetry, stories, her diary or just making lists about ... well anything!! In her darker moments over the past few years, this solitude activity inadvertently brought Louise comfort. It offered the opportunity to come to terms with her thoughts and her grief and it enabled her to bring herself hope and the ability to look towards the horizon with a brighter aspect. Somehow, committing thoughts to paper was a cathartic release for her and adding watercolour sketches allowed her creative mind to soar free and literally bring colour back to the forefront of her mind.

Her guests would be arriving a few days before Christmas, weather permitting, and she had so much house preparation to get done. So with military precision, Louise organized the staff. She spent some time with Betsy in the kitchen going through proposed mealtime dishes. Rose would be an essential help here. Isaac and Jake were charged with venturing out in the appalling weather conditions to bring back food supplies from the village. They rigged up a sledge to facilitate the journey home and seemed quite excited to set out on this particular mission. In the meantime, Violet was instructed to prepare the rooms for the guests and make sure all the linens were immaculate, which Louise knew she would do impeccably.

Louise then set about decorating the house. Tobias was very keen to help out where he could. It was the obvious way to show appreciation for Louise's hospitality and he found that he enjoyed spending time with her and wanted to assist. They decided to bring inside a fir tree to decorate in the salon and that seemed a perfect task for Tobias to take on. So without ado, he togged up in as many suitable clothes as he could from the options Elders could offer and armed with an axe, set out in search of the finest tree.

In the meantime, Izzy was left in Louise's care and the pair sat at the dining table making some dainty posies from the leaves which Louise had gathered a few weeks ago and had been drying in the cellar. Louise showed her how to gather a few pieces together and then helped her to tie a pretty red ribbon around the stems ready to hang on the tree. Louise smiled to herself as she wondered how such a little girl could think of so many questions. Izzy chatted constantly and Louise found herself smiling more than she had done in a long time. Elders brought them a tray of hot milk to enjoy by the fire and some of Betsy's freshly baked warm cake and the pair reveled in the cosiness of the afternoon. Izzy chatted unbidden about her uncle and Louise loved listening to her funny stories. There was so much love there it made her heart melt.

Tobias had not chopped down a tree for Christmas before and felt quite exhilarated about doing so. He smiled to himself, thinking how little attention he had made to developing trends following Prince Albert's introduction of the Christmas tree, almost two decades before. It had become an increasingly more popular annual phenomenon, which no doubt would last a few years longer and then be forgotten like all fashions. Izzy had so much wanted to accompany him but it simply was not suitable to allow her to participate in the adventure this time, as her overclothes were completely unsuitable for such unpredicted and severe weather. In her excitement, however, she had given Tobias strict instructions as to the sort of tree Louise would like. She had taken note of her detailed description and Izzy expected Uncle Tobias to bring the best of examples back. She had never before remembered the joy of a family Christmas with all the trimmings and found the anticipation to be magical.

Tobias walked through heavy drifts, sometimes thigh deep, for some time towards the wooded area just as Louise had directed. He stopped for a moment and turned to take in the magnificent view across the fields and surrounding hills. He could pick out the rooftop of Bancroft House and followed the long tree lined driveway, which lead eventually to the village. He had not known Broadway before this visit but he could understand how Louise was so entranced by it, even with such a cursory glimpse of it from where he stood. He would love to return one day and explore it further. How he wished it could have been different and that Louise had agreed to bring up Izzy and maybe they could have stayed here to live. It would be such a wonderful place to bring up a child. He felt sure Louise could have offered her a loving and secure upbringing... Dismissing his rambling thoughts with a frustrated sigh, he realized the snow had abated just a little and the sun had momentarily pierced the greyness. His eyes could not help but pick out a quite magnificent house nestled into the hillside, perhaps a couple of miles away. He assumed it to be that which belonged to the dubious Mr. Partridge, in all its fine glory. It was certainly an imposing building with extensive land, clearly reaching the perimeter of Bancroft House. Remembering that Louise had said he was newly incumbent and Isaac's advice that he was disrespected locally as an unpleasant man, Tobias wondered about his background and financial substance to support such a property.

Continuing his intended mission, he made his way through the outskirts of the wood, casting a glance at each of the fir trees and assessing their worth versus Izzy's instruction. Again, he smiled to himself. Eventually, he found just the one of which he felt Izzy would approve. Quite tall, fresh green, well balanced branches and an ultimate spike, fine enough to top with a special decoration. He took the axe in hand and with a first swipe, became showered in spraying snow. Absentmindedly, he shrugged it off his shoulders and sleeves, then continued on, to take a further swipe but in doing so, he heard a secondary noise somewhere close by behind him. Mid stoop, he paused like a statue. The noise came again. A sort of whimpering sound. Standing upright and turning slightly to hone in on the sound more specifically, he saw a movement under a tree a few feet away. A dog, curled up, timidly looking up at him with fearful uncertainty but so deeply covered in snow it was hard to distinguish its colour or size. Tobias moved slowly towards it, speaking low and softly so as not to spook the creature. Clearly it had been there some time and made no effort to instinctively move away. Not at all natural. Tobias hesitated, not wishing to spook the dog into biting him, then again moved slowly, crouching this time to lower his eye contact. The dog squeaked a little cry. It was shivering with either anxiety or cold, or both. Tobias spent moments reassuring the creature, gently stroking away the snow then its coarse fur beneath. Tobias tried to encourage it to stand up but it seemed to have difficulty and winced. Constantly speaking in low, soothing whispers, Tobias took a closer look, until he saw a gaping bloody gash across the poor creature's thigh.

Leaving the axe adjacent to the fir tree where it had fallen, Tobias was astonished that the animal allowed him to scoop him up without a grumble and holding him close, they headed back to Bancroft House.

Tobias kicked open the back door into the kitchen with a bang. Betsy, Rose and Elders all snapped up their heads in unison and froze their gaze on the sight before them. The dog was placed with care on the fireside rug and Tobias quickly took off his coat and wrapped it around his find. He asked Rose to fetch some warm water and a cloth to attend to his wound and asked Betsy if she had any milk she could offer the poor creature. Whipping into action they all danced attendance on the canine visitor until his shaking had almost stopped. Isaac came through the door at that moment and hearing that Tobias had rescued a dog in preference to chopping down a Christmas tree, he wrapped a coat around him and followed Tobias's steps in the snow until he came across the half cut tree and axe. He completed the task and dragged it back to the house with Tobias's grateful thanks.

Without any indication of where the dog may have come from or how it had become injured, the necessity to treat his wound was paramount before he could again be let loose.

Izzy thought she might explode with excitement.

"Uncle Tobias… Can I keep him? What is his name? Do you think he likes me? He's so sweet isn't he? Look he's licking my hand. Hahaha", she giggled, "It tickles. Oh! Uncle Tobias I love him" … She looked thoughtful as the dog allowed her to hug him, "I'm going to call him Bouncer because when he's better, he'll be able to bounce around the fields with me!!"

Tobias put his hand across his brow for a fleeting moment,

sighing lightly, wondering how on earth this could escalate so far, so quickly in Izzy's head. Drawing a deep breath and stooping to her level, he began as kindly as possible.

"Izzy, my sweet girl. This poor dog needs our help right now because he has become hurt but he does not belong to us and we cannot claim him as ours. He already has somewhere to live. He will only be allowed to stay at Lady Louise's home until his owner is found and we shall no doubt have gone home ourselves by then, once the snow has lessened. He will already have his own name and probably will be confused by a new name. So, by all means stroke him and show him kindness but please do no think of him as your own. You understand don't you?"

Izzy looked to the floor and with wet eyes, silently nodded. "Good girl" Tobias encouraged, with a ruffle of her hair.

As he stood upright, he caught Louise's eye. She had silently come into the room to see what the fuss was about. Tobias rolled his eyes upwards in indication of a tricky moment with his beloved niece and gestured an apology. She smiled benignly at the situation and felt a pang of warmth in his ever gentle communication with this little girl.

By way of distraction, she added, "Izzy, you'll never guess what Uncle Tobias has also found?!!" Izzy immediately looked up. Louise invitingly held out her hand towards the child and continued, "You must come and see the finest Christmas tree ever!!"

Mr. Partridge stood in his vast library, listening to Thunder's squirming excuses for not delivering on his mission to bring Louise to his master's door. "You're telling me that you had two opportunities to bring me something back and you failed on both scores???? You really are an idiot beyond words! You allowed some random philanthropist to get you drunk and now you don't know even know where the second best is!? She could be working her fingers to the bone right now to make me money and you think excuses are what I want?? No!!! What I wanted in the first place was this Lady Muck to be brought here!!" His fury caused him to sweat profusely and his face reddening more with each syllable spoken. "A little woman got the better of you?? Is that what you're telling me??" Mimicking him absurdly he continued, "Oh she pulled my hair... she screamed in my ear... oh dear me, you poor little thing you!" Back to his gruff voice now, "Do you want to end up where I plucked you from? Shall I have to remind you of your previous job, eh? The workhouse can always take you back you know! Or perhaps the one before that – oh sorry, that wasn't a job, was it? No! That was prison!!! You want me to get you put away again do you?? I have a few little stories to share about you, don't I??" Spitting with fury now he exploded with "Well don't I???" At which point, his wig slipped comically sideways, almost across his eye. Thunder couldn't help himself. He guffawed laughing. Mr. Partridge swung out his right arm and landed his fist right across Thunder's jaw, flattening him to the floor.

Chapter 16

Overnight the snow had stopped completely and was replaced by a cutting, thawing wind. By morning the pale sun had shown itself and the sprawling countryside looked magical. Melting snow was now beginning to drip from the trees and it seemed that the entire world sparkled in the sunlight. The roads were still impassable due to the drifts of compacted snow but at least Tobias and Izzy could plan to take their leave, probably within the next couple of days.

Louise had not heard from her father and she assumed that the atrocious weather had curtailed his travel plans too but assumed his arrival would be imminent once the roads were accessible. As would Aunt Fee's plans. She was so excited to see her dear papa again, although she thought it might be wise not to tell him about the intrusion, for fear of worrying him. She must alert the staff to keep their confidence in this matter. Nevertheless, she did need a serious talk with him. She almost felt angered by his presumptive secrecy and still could not fathom his reasoning. She was impatient to understand why he had clandestinely spoken to Tobias about her potential guardianship of Izzy. They certainly did have a lot to discuss!

All this aside, Louise had to admit that today had been filled with fun and laughter as she and Tobias entertained Izzy – or it may have been Izzy who entertained them?! They took a walk in the gardens and ended up playing games in the snow. It took Louise right back to childhood and that carefree spirit she once knew. Betsy provided wonderful, hearty meals and they spent time sitting by the fire, reading and recounting stories. Louise suddenly remembered that some of her childhood toys or books must be in this house somewhere. There were a couple of places she might ask Violet to hunt them out.

After dinner, Izzy was taken to Rose's room at bedtime, just as had happened the last couple of nights. Tobias and Louise then sat by the fireside in companionable dialogue, exchanging stories of childhood adventures, their upbringing and their aspirations for the future. Tobias confidentially disclosed his ambition, to prevent children from suffering in workhouses. These were not the places for the very young and he described his vision for better care for them with security and education, should their parents fall on hard times. Parents would be relieved to know that their children were at least safely cared for and he felt sure that this in itself would bring them greater tolerance to endure the workhouse themselves. Louise was entranced at how impassioned he was, with such foresight and commitment and she had no doubt at all, that he would achieve his commendable intentions.

Just before they themselves retired, their easy conversation was interrupted when Violet knocked on the door of the salon. She had come to report that Rose was unwell with a fever and Betsy was concerned for her.

Ascertaining that Betsy would remain at Rose's bedside overnight, a brief discussion then ensued between Louise and Tobias, concluding that they must immediately remove Izzy from sharing Rose's room. This was as much for Rose's privacy as Izzy's comfort. Tobias agreed without hesitation, that she be placed on a temporary bed in his room and Louise instructed Violet to achieve this.

There was a scramble of activity until all was accomplished and Izzy was finally fast asleep in her make-do bed. Tobias was so grateful and apologised once more to Louise for all the inconvenience they had brought to her door.

Poor Rose deteriorated overnight despite the experienced care of Betsy, until the decision was made next morning for Louise to call the doctor.

Doctor Gregory arrived later that day to declare that Rose was not the only person in the village to present with such symptoms. He had witnessed over the past week, many people complaining of the same condition and warned that others in this household may suffer the same too. He believed that the symptoms would abate in a few days and in Rose's case, he would not be recommending leeches. However, he did suggest that she be required to take chlorate of potash mixed with spirits of nitre and simple syrup, taken four times a day until she felt better. Familiar with this remedy, Betsy attended to this prescription immediately.

After his consultation, Louise invited the doctor into the parlour offering him a brandy to protect him against the chill outside. As they each took a seat, Doctor Gregory conversationally remarked upon the convalescing dog in front of the fire adding that he felt sure he recognised it. Tobias recounted the story of his rescue and this confirmed the doctor's suspicion that he belonged to Mr. Partridge from the neighbouring estate. Interestingly, he then added that it was of no surprise to him, if his injuries were also inflicted by his master.

Tobias was astounded by his comment and was now beginning to understand why Mr. Partridge's reputation had gone before him! Tobias cautiously navigated the dialogue to purge as much information as possible from the doctor about Mr. Partridge, without Louise suspecting his intent. With very little encouragement, it easily became apparent that Doctor Gregory considered him an obnoxious man who treated his animals as violently as his staff. Louise was appalled and could not fathom the mentality of any master who could run a household on violence and fear. She truly thought those dark days were history.

It was then that the doctor made a complete aside, which took them both by surprise. He added that his own concern was greater for those he employed in his workhouse. He himself was the doctor who was routinely called in to care for those too sick to work or the very elderly who were housed in the infirmary attached to Broadside Workhouse, some few miles away.

Tobias visibly paled as he recognised the name. Dear Lord! The very same as where he found Izzy. Seething with anger, he realised that the man he had been searching for, was on this very doorstep. Louise cast him a knowing glance. She interjected and deliberately digressed from the conversation, stepping towards the door in invitation for the doctor to take his leave, whilst assuring him of Rose's best care, as he exited.

After barely any sleep, Tobias announced at breakfast that he had urgent business to attend to and he would very much appreciate it, if he could presume upon Louise to leave Izzy in her care for a short while, while he wrote some letters ready to be sent to the post once the snow had cleared. It was not difficult for Louise to determine what this business might involve and if she was right in her assumptions, she was rather concerned for his safety. Yet, without hesitation, Louise asked Betsy to allow Izzy to do some baking with her to keep her occupied. Izzy was invited to stir the Christmas pudding and she had made a special wish, which she refused to share with anyone, as she said it would not come true otherwise.

Louise was quite grateful for some time to concentrate on some of her own business. Spending some time at her desk was what she needed to take her mind off the strange turn of events unfolding in front of her. By the time Tobias appeared for dinner and Izzy had proudly presented the cakes she and Betsy had been baking, a calm had returned to the household.

Mr. Partridge kicked his bonehead lackey in the ribs and with a groan he came back to life. You have one more chance. If you fail me – you're in real trouble. With that, he strode out of the room slamming the door behind him. The shudder almost put out the fire and Thunder felt the vibration go through his body.

As the sun rose the following morning, the snow had cleared significantly and Tobias announced that he and Izzy planned to leave the following morning, once the roads were again safe for the carriage. He hoped Louise could possibly accommodate them one last evening. For this, he would be very grateful.

For today, however, Tobias had a further request from Louise. He wondered if he could ask Isaac to accompany him for a short while. "I want to return Bouncer – erm the dog to his rightful owner." He laughed to himself that despite his best efforts the dog's new name had stuck! "It is my duty to see if Mr. Partridge has indeed lost his dog. Isaac knows the area well, so I should not get lost!! My own driver could take over his duties in his absence, if you would allow it, Louise."

Louise had come to consider Isaac as a sensible lad and agreed he was the best person to accompany Tobias, so gladly gave her permission. Without him needing to ask further, Louise suggested that Izzy stayed at Bancroft House. Tobias had hoped she would offer this, as he was not sure what the day would hold and yet again hated such imposition but was so appreciative of her kindly cooperation.

After breakfast, Tobias told Izzy to say her goodbyes to Bouncer. Through floods of tears, the little girl hugged her new canine friend and in turn he licked her face repeatedly. Violet did her best to distract her whilst the dog had a loop of rope tied around its neck and was taken from the kitchen.

Violet took Izzy to pay a visit to Rose, who was slowly

beginning to recover in bed. Rose was shocked to see the tearful child and despite feeling terrible herself, invited her to sit on her bed and allowed her to offload her sorrow of losing Bouncer. They hugged, as Rose commiserated with her sad tale and Violet left them together for a short while. Once she heard Izzy resuming her laughter, she rescued Rose from the energetic child and let her rest again.

Isaac had configured a short cut across the fields and they picked up a steady pace with the dog slightly limping but keeping up, despite his sore limb. The path they took followed Louise's land then passed by the wood where Jake had been working that fateful day. Isaac suggested jumping the fence and traversing the neighbour's wood, to cut off a significant corner.

Tobias was uneasy about trespassing and would rather have approached the property from the front sweeping drive but the cold was beginning to bite and so he agreed. Between them, they lifted the dog over the fence and continued their walk through the tangled wood whereupon the dog's manner seemed to immediately change, with his nose to the ground in recognition. Tobias felt sure he was on familiar ground.

They caught sight of the stone house through the trees but needed to circumnavigate the thickness of undergrowth to exit the wood. Bouncer suddenly stopped and yanked Tobias back towards a place of interest a few feet away. Tobias tried to tug him away but the dog was insistent. Trying again to gently pull the dog away from his find, Tobias was now getting frustrated with the creature, as he started to dig at the partially melted slushy snow. Cursing now, he spoke firmly to the dog, nudging him with his knee away from his mission.

The dog however, was not for moving and began to bark as he dug more determinedly. Huffing with exasperation, Tobias was about to physically lift the dog away when with a sharp flick of soil from his scraping paw, a porcelain white emaciated hand, flicked out and flopped lifelessly forward. The dog's intent increased and within a moment, he had excavated a whole clothed arm.

Isaac and Tobias exchanged a frantic look of horror. Fear sparked between them. Thinking quickly, Tobias needed the dog to be quiet. All this barking was going to draw attention. They must not be caught here. With a silent signal to Isaac, they frantically covered up the skin and bones with the newly raked earth and yanked the excited dog back along the way they came. Rapidly retracing their steps, they jumped the fence and without a second's hesitation, they desperately passed the dog one to the other and hurriedly trod the snow back to the sanity of Bancroft House without pausing for breath.

Izzy was beside herself with joy to be unexpectedly reunited with Bouncer and Tobias had no time to quell her excitement. He headed straight to find Louise, whilst Isaac babbled the horrific story to his shocked downstairs colleagues. Jake ran outside and around the corner to be sick. Violet threw her hands to her face with a screech of horror. Rose lapped up the gossip and Betsy flustered about trying to calm everyone. Elders said little but took a tray of brandy and two glasses upstairs, suspecting it was badly needed.

What to do next was the biggest problem.

Chapter 17

Next morning, Rose was much improved but sadly, Izzy had taken ill during the night too. Betsy and Violet had their hands full trying to keep them both attended to, in addition to their daily chores.

Louise's priority right now was to ensure Izzy was nursed better. She herself ensured the child had warm water to gargle with and the same linctus as that prepared for Rose, was also to be administered. Both tasks needed patience as the gargling was tricky to teach her to do and the medicine tasted vile. She sat with her for hours at a time, cooling her forehead and stroking her hair, talking soothingly to her until she slipped once more into unsettled sleep.

In the meantime, after much consideration, Tobias decided he may need the expertise of a barrister to assist him in his quest to bring Mr. Partridge to justice. Things were looking very wrong and dangerous and despite the difficult five or six mile trudge through the wet snow into the neighbouring town of Evesham, he must consult an expert. On his way back through Broadway, he would report his findings and express his concerns to the police. There was no official police station in this country village but a small police 'house' held a single cell and at the most two police officers could be found on duty. This was not known as an area of great crime but petty theft and incidents of unruliness through over-imbibing at the hostelries were about the most excitement that they dealt with.

Tobias's errand would realistically take the best part of the day. So with clear directions, he set off as soon as possible after breakfast. He hated to leave Izzy in such a poorly state but this business was urgent and he believed the safety of all of them was a priority. He also knew that Izzy was in the best possible care.

Word reached the kitchen that Mr. Woolmer was going to report the incident to the Police. Elders approved wholeheartedly and Rose thought it the most exciting thing ever. Betsy however, was more worried that Jake was falling ill too. His demeanour was very odd – not at all like Rose or Izzy's symptoms but he had become ghostly white in complexion and she noticed he was refusing food and constantly on edge and fidgety. Elders shared her concern and sought Lady Louise's opinion. Hearing their misgivings, she suggested that after the servant's tea had been served, Jake should be sent to the parlour to assist her in a task. She needed to form her own opinion.

Violet too had seen the change in Jake. He was not at all himself – in fact he had not been so for some days. She thought back and concluded it was since the day he had that awful experience near the wood. She felt so sorry for him and wondered what she could do to help. At lunchtime, she contrived to sit beside him. He was picking at the food put before him with disinterest. Violet started to chat about something funny that had happened that morning with Izzy, as generally that would make Jake laugh. They generally shared the same sense of humour. Worryingly though, she could see her chatter was annoying him and so she curtailed her story.

Betsy went to collect something from the pantry and for a brief moment they were left alone before Isaac and Rose came in from the byre. "What ever is the matter, Jake?" she said gently, almost whispering. "Please do not say 'nothing', because I know there is" She hesitated, "and I worry about you!" Jake looked at her in astonishment. "Well you should not care for me, Violet!" he admonished. Violet made to speak again but he stopped her abruptly. "Violet... you deserve me to tell the truth, so I will." Her heart thumped a beat, "I'm listening.... what is it? Are you truly ill?"

"Violet, you should not wish to talk to me if I tell you."

She wanted to interrupt but sensing this, he stopped her with a raised hand. He could not look at her. He looked at his plate of food and blurted out, "You must not care for me, Violet. I am not a good man, Violet. I am in trouble."

Hearing Isaac coming towards the door, he quickly added, "You must not tell anyone Violet. Promise me." His eyes pleaded with hers and her throat constricted to prevent the tears. She nodded assurance that it was their secret. Whatever it was that was disconcerting Jake, it was making him ill. She must be patient and wait for him to disclose more, for she was not going to let this go. This was not the time to press him further but she must find the opportunity to do so. She needed to be able to help him.

It was Violet's turn now to lose her appetite but she was inventive enough to distract herself and initiate inane conversation with Isaac. Jake continued to silently play with his food but was fortunately rescued by Elders' instruction to attend to Lady Louise in the parlour. He gladly scooted back his chair, scraping it across the stone floor and almost ran from the kitchen.

"What's up with him then?" asked Isaac with surprise. "He's been proper moody lately." Violet shrugged indifferently and passed over a plate of warm scones. In desperation for a change of subject, finally Violet told her a funny story about Izzy.

Louise needed a little time to spend with Jake to understand what was going on. She too had noticed his look of something indefinable – maybe something like worry or even distress but she had dismissed her thoughts believing he was just readjusting to life at Bancroft House. Maybe he was homesick for the town house or finding his new responsibilities too much. She hated to think he may be sad but could not imagine him admitting to this lightly.

Suddenly an idea occurred to her, which would kill two birds with one stone. It would provide an opportunity for her to share time with Jake as well as creating an early Christmas gift for Izzy. Since Izzy had become poorly, it was quite clear that their departure intentions would yet again be compromised. It was so very near Christmas now and Aunt Fee and Uncle Gerald would be arriving within the next couple of days. Two more guests would make little difference and sending Izzy home in the cold on a long journey when she was still convalescing, would be very unkind. She decided that inviting Tobias and Izzy to stay a few more days over the Christmas season, until Izzy was completely better, would indeed be a Christian thing to do.

With that, she explained her project to Jake and under her careful instruction, he set to with Louise's plan to resurrect the room adjacent to the one in which Tobias was staying. He began to clear the bedroom, which once belonged to Louise as a child, whilst she sat upon the bed and chatted her instructions. She noticed that Jake was very guarded and somewhat uncomfortable in her presence, which was most unlike the Jake she knew.

Approaching the subject, Louise asked him how he was settling into life at Bancroft House and he said it was "very nice" but when she then asked if he preferred to be here or back at her father's town house, he almost jumped at what he thought was an offer to return there. Confused, she asked him why. Not satisfied with his non-committal comment about not liking the countryside, she challenged him further. "Jake, I remember you seemed to be fine before that day you had that incident with our neighbour's groundsman. What really happened that day?"

Jake froze and the pulse in his forehead was visibly throbbing as his heart rate increased. "Ma'am, I'd rather not talk about this, Ma'am…" he repeated himself nervously. Not letting the subject go, Louise pushed him further, 'Jake, I know you better than this! Something is the matter! I believe you are frightened of something. Are you sure you told me everything? Did that man in the wood threaten you more than you're telling me, Jake?"

Jake turned his back in pretence of moving another chair but Louise moved towards him, placing her hand on his arm to impair his movement. "Jake! Look at me!!" she commanded. "JAKE!", she repeated more firmly. Slowly, the young lad turned towards her, his eyes blinking to prevent a tear. "Please tell me what this is about Jake. I hope to be able to help you. Whatever this is, it is making you ill."

Jake took a deep breath and began, "Ma'am, the man I saw in the woods…. I saw him again in the big house." He looked at his Ladyship directly in the eyes and tried to find the words but seeing her naive and sweet kindness, his courage failed him. How could he possibly confess that he'd buried a murdered body?!

He had to try. Beginning again, "Ma'am, he's a bully and …"

A knock came to the door and Violet popped her head around to see what she could do next to help. The moment had gone and Jake was strangely relieved to be interrupted. Frustrated at the timing of this intrusion, Louise quietly reassured Jake of her understanding, she told him to continue with his work as best as he could, to get the room sorted. She would have to leave this be for the moment.

There were many items of furniture to be removed from what had become a storeroom and the remainder required rearranging as directed. The plan took all afternoon to execute and Louise was constantly popping in and out to check on Izzy's recovery. Betsy and Violet took turns also in attending to her. Once this heavy work was achieved, Violet then dusted off the rocking horse, shelves and curtains and Louise added the final touches to make the room just as enchanting as she had remembered it as a child.

Jake made up the fire to warm the room. By the time they had finished, the room looked altogether wonderfully cosy and fit for a princess. Louise made Violet and Jake keep her secret, just for the time being.

Chapter 18

Louise felt uneasy that Tobias had still not appeared back home by early afternoon.

The sun was lowering in the sky already and Louise could not imagine why Tobias had taken so long. Izzy had asked for him a number of times but the staff and Louise had reassured her he would be back shortly. The little girl was very unwell and the responsibility of caring for her in Tobias's absence, greatly concerned Louise. Touchingly, when she had last looked in on her, Louise had found Bouncer sitting by her bedside, as though in prayer, his head resting on his crossed front paws, close to her chest. His doleful eyes were almost pleading for her speedy recovery.

By the time Elders brought her liquid refreshment at three o'clock, she felt sure something was amiss. The sun was lowering in the sky and she wondered if perhaps Tobias had mistaken his route home and simply got lost. She called for Isaac to come to her. Explaining her concerns, she instructed him to walk into the village to see if he could find Mr. Woolmer. On the assumption that he must by now have reached Broadway from Evesham, she hoped that Isaac would meet Mr. Woolmer on the way back to Bancroft House. If he did not, then she suggested that Isaac should ask at the police building to ascertain what time Mr. Woolmer had left. She desperately hoped that he had somehow just mislaid his route home. Issac left immediately, feeling sure that the house guest would be found just a short distance from Bancroft House.

Tobias had indeed reached the police house. He quickly regaled to the on duty sergeant, the entire story of finding the injured dog, treating his wounds and attempting to return it to his rightful owner. He hated to admit to cutting across Mr. Partridge's land in an attempt to shorten the distance of his errand, especially since he could technically be accused of trespassing but he needed to explain his full story in order to divulge his grotesque find.

Isaac, reached the village without a sign of Mr. Woolmer and thought that perhaps he had taken the occasion to purchase something from the post office store. Indeed, when he enquired within, Isaac was informed that they had had a fine gentleman customer in the shop much earlier today. Issac, however, could not understand why he had still not reached home. The only option left was, as Lady Louise had instructed, to ask at the police station.

Approaching the station from the side, Isaac, hearing raised voices, stopped short of the door. Alarmingly, he recognized Mr. Woolmer's voice forcefully trying to correct the other man's accusations. Isaac crept forward to find a low, barred window and stealthily tried to get vision through the corner of the glass. Mr. Woolmer was in full view, looking very agitated and concerned. The police officer had his back to Isaac and was shouting above Mr. Woolmer. It seemed like they were having a terrible argument. Isaac was about to go in but just then Mr. Woolmer's attention was taken by his movement at the door and distracting the officer for a slight moment, gestured silently for Isaac to stay away.

Confused for a moment, Isaac darted back momentarily away from the window, only to creep forward again and see the officer reach into his belt to release a pair of hand cuffs, shouting something about "...arresting you for the mur....". Mr. Woolmer's panicked remonstrations made it impossible to hear clearly but Isaac could have sworn the officer said ...murder???

Surely not! There was a slight struggle as Mr. Woolmer resisted arrest but the police officer had Mr. Woolmer's hands behind his back and thrust him towards an internal door. They both disappeared.

Isaac ran through the now wet snow, faster than he had ever needed to run before, back to the house. Dragging his breath, he asked Elders' permission to speak with Lady Louise urgently, then stammered through what he had witnessed to both her Ladyship and Elders. "I was going to go in m'Lady but Mr. Woolmer signaled for me to go away." Explained Isaac.

"No, Isaac, you did the right thing. I believe Mr. Woolmer would not want you to become embroiled in all of this and needed you to raise the alarm here! You did well Isaac. Go and get Betsy to make you a hot drink." Isaac left the room feeling flustered and rather shaken.

Turning to her father's trusted butler, Louise looked for a semblance of calm wisdom, "Oh Elders, this is terrible!! Do you think he has been accused of murdering the poor soul they found in the woods?"

She paced frantically up and down the hallway, screwing her hands together tightly. "What are we going to do, Elders??

Nothing could be done that night. They must sleep on it and consider the best move to make in the morning.

Louise sent Violet to sit with Izzy and should the child ask after her uncle, she must be told he has had to go to a meeting and will be back. She was also instructed to keep her aware of her wellbeing. At least Rose had improved enough to get back to work tomorrow, doing some small but helpful tasks.

On reflection, Tobias thought he could maybe have phrased things differently, or even not come here at all! Before he knew it, he was being manhandled towards a stinking cell, fighting against being arrested on suspicion of murder. How could this possibly be happening?

Louise looked about her home, comfortable and cosy in its Christmas decoration and could not consider the dreadful conditions in which Mr. Woolmer had found himself this evening. At least, she hoped he knew that Izzy would be well cared for and that they would do all they could to have him released. But how??

It was as though the day had suddenly caught up on Louise. She slumped in a chair with her head in her hands when a sudden thought occurred to her. "Oh my life!" she said to herself. "Aunt Fee is coming tomorrow!!!"...

Chapter 19

After barely any sleep, the day dawned early for Louise. Violet came to assist her to dress then returned to do what she could in the kitchen under Betsy's instruction, in anticipation of the travelling guests. Jake had his work cut out first thing with the fires and fortunately Violet had already got all the necessary accommodation prepared for the guests and Rose was already setting the dining room table for their arrival later in the day.

It was with much relief that Izzy was found to be a little improved after a good night's sleep. She was taking the medicine without fuss and still trying her best to gargle although her actions were somewhat comedic, even to herself. It was good to hear her little giggle had returned but she was still very weak and pale. She was well enough to enjoy a picture book for short moments at a time to occupy herself but she was still very weary and slept a good deal, either side of being tempted with a little food.

Louise worried about Tobias. How could she possibly help him? She did not wish to worry her father and in any case a message would take time to reach him and time was of the essence. She really needed this to be sorted by the time her father came to stay. She wondered how he would deal with this, if he were here.

She concluded that he would advise her to look logically at all the information before her. She found herself considering all that she knew or suspected about her neighbour. Mr. Partridge had a reputation as an unpleasant, violent and bullying man. She now knew, thanks to the doctor, that he was guardian of a workhouse. A body had been found in his grounds. In addition, Isaac was a witness to the unearthing of the body – but if he took this information to the police to support Tobias, he too could be damned for his murder, if they were not careful. She assumed that this was why Tobias did not wish to involve him, as he himself anticipated arrest. There had been an intrusion into her home. Someone had tried to abduct her...and why would anyone wish to kidnap Rose? And then there was Jake... she could not shake off her concerns about Jake.

Louise needed to talk to him again... There was something more to this. She sent for him to come directly to the salon where she again found herself pacing the room. With little preamble, she approached him directly about his recent encounter and demanded he tell her the entire truth. Jake had already heard from Isaac that Mr. Woolmer had likely been arrested in connection with the body and knew that he could hide this story no longer.

"Ma'am..." he finally began... "I have done something really bad." Louise was taken aback. She really did not expect this turn of events. Jake had always been a solid kind of character and realised that this must be very serious. "I'm listening. Tell me."

Jake sat on the nearest chair, uninvited. His legs had threatened not to hold him any longer. He put his head in his shaking hands and cried unashamedly. Louise put an encouraging hand on his shoulder with a slight squeeze. "Come along, tell me Jake."

Taking a deep breath, Jake began his sorry story whilst Louise sat in silence, listening intently. He could manage but a few sentences at a time before his voice broke again or he took another shakily deep breath, to enable him to continue. His narrative sounded, even to himself, like a surreal episode in a book. It was his own living nightmare. Once his purgative monologue was over, he sighed a deep relief. Immediately, he felt gratifyingly better for sharing his darkest secret.

Louise sat dumbfounded for several moments after Jake had finished speaking. The silence hung uncomfortably between them. There was something about Jake's description of this man that profoundly troubled Louise. Could he really be the same vile person who had entered her home? A murderer?? Louise faltered at this realisation.

Recalling then that Rose had mentioned her abductor's threat to take her to the workhouse as an appeasement for his boss. Could that be her neighbour? She felt instantly sick at the possibility and wondered how many others had been 'stolen to order' to augment his task force for his own financial gain? Was this man truly working for Mr. Partridge?

One by one, they were all becoming embroiled in this horror story, all of which emanated from Mr. Partridge.

She wished Tobias was here.

The roadway was now just about passable on foot, so Louise decided to wrap up warm and make her way directly to the police house. Elders begged her not to go but she was stubbornly insistent.

Entering the police building, she asked to see the officer in charge. Shocked to see Lady Dorchester, they fussed about correcting their ties and brushing off imaginary fluff from their blue uniforms. The older of the two gentlemen present, stepped forward asking how he could be of assistance.

With a straight back and head high, Louise questioned as brusquely as she could muster, belying the stomach churning nervousness inside. "I believe you are holding a Mr. Woolmer here. Is that correct?"

"Indeed we do." Came the shocked response.

"Good!" she affirmed. "Well I should like you to show me the way please. It is important I see him."

"Ma'am, I do not think that is a good idea."

"I beg your pardon, Sir?"

"Mr. Woolmer is suspected of being a very dangerous man, Ma'am. I cannot recommend you see him."

"And on what do you base your accusations, Sir?" she asked with authority.

"Well Ma'am, he has all but confessed, Ma'am."

"To whom did he confess, Sir?"

"Well to my assistant, here Ma'am."

"Well, Sir, I should very much like it if you would bring the accused here right now, as I should like to hear for myself, his confession."

Shrugging his shoulders he continued, "I do not think th.."

"NOW!!" Louise repeated harshly.

"Yes, Ma'am. Straight away Ma'am."

Moments lapsed. Louise neither moved nor spoke a word. The assistant police officer did similarly.

"Lady Dorchester!!" came Tobias's shocked voice!! "What on earth are you doing here?!" then added "Is my niece alright? Is she worse?"

Following his lead in sounding formal, "Mr. Woolmer, do not concern yourself about your niece."

Trying to distract herself from his dishevelled state, she turned to the officer and asked, "Please inform me of what Mr. Woolmer is accused."

"He has been arrested on suspicion of murder, Ma'am."

"Is that so? She raised her eyebrows and looked at him mockingly. "Have you interviewed this man yourself?"

"Erm, no not yet, Ma'am, I...."

"Are you telling me Sir, that you have locked up a man, on the authority of your assistant and taken his word that he is suspected of murder?"

Jittering with the unexpected challenge, "I er... I am ... er about to..."

Impatiently Louise interjected his stammering, "And who is Mr. Woolmer alleged to have murdered, Sir?"

Seemingly embarrassed, the officer replied, "Well we do not have the body as yet Ma'am?'

"You do not have a body but you are accusing this man of murder?"

"We believe he has buried the body ..."

Cutting across his response, Louise asked, "And where do you believe this body is buried?"

"We believe in the grounds of Mr. Partridge's home Lady Louise."

"And why do you believe that, Sir?"

"Because, Mr. Woolmer told us and..."

"Do you honestly believe he would tell you where there is a dead body, if he had killed a man? HUMMM?" She pulled the cuffs of her glove a little higher in a dramatic pause. "That is rather too presumptuous, do you not think Sir?"

Turning now to Tobias, she continued, "Mr. Woolmer, I should very much like to hear your confession – whatever that might be. Please do tell!"

Tobias tried to assess this cold front Louise was portraying but was uncertain if this was for real or for the benefit of the police officers.

"Lady Dorchester, I have made no such confession. I came here as a good citizen in search of advice and protection and my story has been misconstrued. I was handcuffed and taken to a cell on a false assumption."

Louise took advantage of his statement, "Mr. Woolmer, are you willing to swear on oath that you have not committed a crime?"

"Indeed Lady Dorchester, I swear on my niece's life."

Turning to the officer in charge, "I think you will find, Sir, that you are holding this man without evidence or confession. I can personally vouch for this man's good honour and I suggest that you free him immediately. Do you understand me?"

Seeing the officer twitch with uncertainty, she flicked up her dainty hand into the air as though swiping away a wasp, "This is preposterous in the extreme and I shall be sure that Lord Dorchester will be reporting this to your superiors.... Might I remind you, that my father is very influential in these parts and he will be most disenchanted to hear of this ludicrous pantomime."

Walking away from the whole fiasco, Louise could barely believe that the officer in charge had released Tobias and even added a personal apology. Even less could she conceive where her inner strength had come from and as they both left the station, she could scarcely credit that her temerity had paid off.

Trekking home to Bancroft House, Tobias found the feistiness of this lovely lady beside him, intriguing. He had never witnessed such strength of character in a young woman and he had to admit to himself that with every passing day, he admired her more and more. If he only admitted it to himself, it was more than that. He found himself entranced by her - her determination, her loyalty, her courage, her sweet giggle when she played with Izzy.... She was truly a special lady.

The pathway was still a little slippery and so Tobias offered his hand on the pretence of assisting Louise but even when the narrow lane was completely devoid of peril, they continued to walk quite naturally arm in arm, until they reached the house. He carried a large paper parcel wrapped with string in his other hand. Seeing Louise look questioningly at it, he confided he had at least managed to purchase a few Christmas gifts for Izzy from the village, before his nightmare had begun.

Yet again, feeling enormous relief in his freedom, his thanks seemed so inadequate, yet she accepted it with such good-natured grace and geniality.

He teased her performance of pluck and impertinence in her dealing with the sergeant and re-enacting the scenario between them, they laughed like children and could not wait to get home to enjoy a restorative brandy by the fire.

Violet told Izzy that uncle Tobias was home and she sat patiently waiting for him to come to her little make-do cot bed, still set up in his room. Tobias had shaved and scrubbed up clean to rid himself of the stench of the cell. The little girl squealed with excitement to see her uncle back and suddenly found the energy to tell him about how poorly she had been and how Betsy had made her some special 'get better' soup which had worked and she felt so much better. She wanted to show him how she had learnt to gargle but he managed to defer that experience for another day.

Louise joined them and believing that Tobias deserved a room to himself again with some peace and privacy after his ordeal, suggested that since Izzy was also feeling a little better, she might like to have an early Christmas gift. With huge anticipation and still very wobbly on her legs, Louise offered her hand and led her to the connecting door leading to the adjacent room. As she swung open the door, Izzy let out a little yelp of joy. Her eyes widened so much that Louise thought they may pop out and she let out a gasp of wonderment.

Tracking her eyes around the room, Louise watched as she took in all that was before her. Izzy looked up into Louise's eyes for an explanation. Louise stooped down beside this sweet little girl and whispered, "Would you like to sleep in here until you are feeling well enough to go home Izzy? This used to be my room when I was a little girl. Perhaps when you are well enough tomorrow you can look at some of my books and there are some games in there too," she pointed to an old trunk in the corner of the cosy room. The pale little girl held up her arms in thanks to Louise, who squeezed her gently in response. Standing back up, Louise gently directed Izzy towards the newly made pink, counterpaned bed and helped her into it. The child snuggled down in blissful comfort and Louise knew she would soon be asleep.

Tobias stepped forward and crooned some soothing words and kissed her gently on the top of her head as he always did. "Get some rest dear child. You are still quite unwell. I shall pop in again later before I myself retire."

She looked at him with sheepish eyes, coughed a little and said "Uncle Tobias, please may I ask Lady Louise for a kiss too?" Without time for him to reply, Louise's throat constricted with emotion as she stepped forward from Tobias's side and bent over his niece, placing a kiss on her cheek. "You will feel better tomorrow little one," she smiled encouragingly, "You'll see!"

Tobias was overwhelmed by her loving kindness. They both moved to exit the door when a little voice added "Lady Louise.... Thank you!"...

Just at that moment, a furry creature brushed gently passed Louise's skirts and head hanging a little low for fear of being scolded, silently approached Izzy's bed and flopped beside her, devotedly. Tobias raised his eyebrows and with a shrug of his shoulders, looked to Louise questioningly. She smiled and nodded her approval. Izzy was already asleep.

Chapter 20

A moderate carriage swept up the drive and a rather loud, garrulous, overweight woman was helped down the awkward carriage step. Louise held her breath, thinking that at any moment she might land on top of poor Isaac and crush him to death. A bumbling gentleman followed in her wake, somewhat insignificantly, as the woman commanded so much attention that he was barely noticed.

"Aunt Fee! How wonderful to see you again! Welcome!" Turning her attention to Uncle Gerald she was about to greet him too but Aunt Fee had already tugged on Louise's arm using her as purchase to climb the few stone steps towards the open front doorway. Thus distracted, Louise was caused to simply acknowledge Uncle Gerald over her shoulder, with a smile and a simple word of greeting. Without drawing breath, the elderly lady was seamlessly asking at least five consecutive questions about the house, intermingled with memories of previous visits and complaining of how cold she was. Louise had barely a second to even ask after their journey but eyed to Elders to make sure Uncle Gerald was following and managing the steps too.

Guiding Aunt Fee to the nearest chair as she had already requested, she sank ungraciously into it, her weight pushing the chair back against the wall with a crack. Louise had no idea, whether it was the legs or the back of the chair, which had broken but hoped that either way, it would support her weight! Aunt Fee needed to catch her wheezing breath and Louise was tempted to ask her simply not to speak for a moment to recover but her incapacity did not seem to quell her desire to continue chattering. After a short moment, using her silver topped cane to give her purchase to stand, she asked for Louise to catch her opposite arm and with a tug, raised herself off the broken chair, almost pulling Louise to the ground in the process.

Leading Aunt Fee to the parlour, she was then lowered into a more sumptuous Chesterfield and Uncle Gerald following obediently behind, Elders suggested a tray of refreshments would be brought immediately. The fire roared up the chimney with its inviting warming flames licking up the chimney but Aunt Fee still exaggerated a shiver and rubbed her gnarled fingers together in disappointment. "Is there a draught in her, my dear? I feel my feet are white with cold."

Louise picked up a soft woollen shawl she sometimes wrapped herself in and caringly placed it across Aunt Fee's knees. "Oh darling that is so much better. I'm sure I shall be more comfortable after our hot refreshments!" She added. "I usually find a good brandy fixes things, don't you dear??"

Taking the hint, Louise rang the bell and asked a bobbing Rose to please bring the best cognac for her guests, immediately. Turning again to Uncle Gerald, Louise shook his hand with a gracious welcome but realised quite rapidly that he was almost entirely deaf. Shouting now, he could apparently get the gist of her cordiality and replied "Yes my dear, I'll have a large glass if you please." Perplexed, Louise smiled. The refreshments arrived.

After some forty minutes of imbibing most of the precious cognac and very little food, Aunt Fee requested she be taken to her room for a lie down and tub bath before dinner. Violet was dispatched to assist in all that Aunt Fee might require. Similarly, Jake was charged with accompanying Uncle Gerald to assist with his needs.

Louise fell back inelegantly into her favourite chair with relief and fatigue. She had barely had her guests an hour. She had a sense that dinner would be exhausting!

Tobias came down shortly afterwards. He had been sitting with Izzy for a short while, reading to her from one of Louise's childhood books. Inside the front cover of the chosen book, Izzy had noticed a handwritten note, which she asked Tobias to read to her. "To my darling Louise, on your sixth birthday. With much love, always and forever." Signed, Mamma.

Izzy was entranced by this. "Do all mammas give their little girls books uncle Tobias?" Tobias considered his response. "Mmm, some do ... I'm sure your dear Mamma would have gifted you lots of books if she had been able to ... she liked books - just like you do!!" "And would she have written 'To my darling Izzy with much love always and forever?" Tobias hugged her just a little and assured her "I am certain she would have done that, my dear. I know she loves you always and forever." Satisfied with his answer, she was keen to read the book and snuggled up against him to listen to his comforting tones.

Louise rolled her eyes as he walked in the room. He smiled. "Problem?"

"No, not really! I had just forgotten how tiring Aunt Fee can be!" She laughed at herself. I must get changed now for dinner. You will join us, won't you?" she almost begged.

"I don't wish to impose, Louise. Perhaps I ought not..."

"Tobias, I'd really appreciate it if you would. It would really take the pressure off from me, conversationally!!" They both laughed.

Thunder had decided he would hover outside Bancroft House to observe the comings and goings and assess the risk of entering the house to capture his target. Last time was easy: The staff was largely absent. However, today looked busy. It was dark outside now and the house was fully candlelit as though they were having a party. He wasn't sure this was good timing at all. Sometimes however, lots of activity and alcohol reduces people's awareness - he had learnt this for himself! Also, noise could be a great distraction. He needed to be patient, so sneaked in amongst some bushes in front of the dining room, perched himself on bended knee and watched.

The house looked divine. So special and Christmassy - even romantic. Louise was delighted with the effect she had created. Aunt Fee waddled down the stairs, hips swinging her glittering frock from side to side, as the candlelight caught the beading. She began her monologue before she had even reached the middle of the staircase.

Uncle Gerald was already sitting in the salon with a large glass of cognac in his hand, twisting the glass repeatedly between his aged fingers, admiring its amber fluidity. He thought there were few things more beautiful.

Once Aunt Fee had ensconced herself in the mirror image chair, Elders approached her with a tray. Pouring a small brandy for her enjoyment, the elderly lady surreptitiously placed her finger beneath the bottle to tip it further. A splash more brandy shot into the glass and she grabbed it before Elders could apologise or even worse, retract it. Louise had not even managed to interrupt her babble, enough to politely compliment her on her gown. The woman simply didn't seem to draw breath! She was beginning to feel that this was going to be a long evening.

Just then, a gentle knock on the door heralded the sight of Tobias. He entered the room with such masculine composure, it quite took Louise's breath away. "Good evening" he announced to nobody in particular. Louise introduced her house guest as the son of her father's legal adviser who was on business in the area and also staying a few days. For the first time since she arrived, Aunt Fee stopped talking and gawped at the extremely handsome figure in front of her, mouth wide open. Heaven knows what was going through her mind but Louise found it quite amusing. Tobias put out his hand in gesture for her to remain seated and extended the other to gently take hers. He tipped his head forward and planted a pretence of a kiss on her knuckles, which she received with a flustered giggle. She rapidly grabbed her fan and erratically wafted it around, catching her nose in it as she did so.

With elegant ease, Tobias led the conversation asking Uncle Gerald as many questions and Aunt Fee in equal order. Uncle Gerald did not seem quite so deaf and Louise put this down to the resonance of his voice and was relieved. Astonishingly too, Aunt Fee did not interrupt once and Tobias had a real knack of interjecting to prevent her ramblings.

The dinner gong rang and in the most charming manner, Tobias held out his arm as invitation for Aunt Fee to link him as he escorted her towards the dining room. He glanced at Louise with what she thought was a wink of his eye and she bit her tongue to stop herself laughing at Aunt Fee's haughty acquiescence.

Aunt Fee and Uncle Gerald took their seats and Tobias held the chair for Louise before he himself was seated. Aunt Fee was certainly enamoured by the young man sharing their table. She managed to fire many questions at Tobias and in fact Louise was learning quite a good deal about him. The evening was passing with a comfortable, convivial atmosphere and Betsy had done them proud with the delicious dishes she had produced.

Aunt Fee could not have failed to have had a wonderful evening but she was not inclined to say so. Rather she kept reminding Louise of the 'old days' and the perfection her mother had achieved. Louise loved the stories of those days of course but she also felt a slight disappointment that Aunt Fee had not thought to show appreciation for all her efforts today. She was, however, effusive in her attention towards Tobias. It was quite clear that she thought it was her place to match make between him and Louise and went to embarrassing levels to demonstrate her thoughts. Aunt Fee was certainly loose tongued with alcohol and there were moments when Louise wished she herself were not there. It did however amuse Tobias to realize she would not look him in the eye, during these episodes. As a diversion from the awkwardness, Louise announced to Rose who was delivering the food that she intended to serve dessert. They had worked hard and should finish tasks in the kitchens and take an early night. Elders could follow up later with the brandy.

Just as the desserts were about to be served, there was a knock at the door and Violet presented herself apologetically, requesting Mr. Woolmer go to Izzy, as she'd had a nightmare and would not settle without him. He made profuse apologies and left the room, insisting they continued without him. She had not had one of these nightmares in some time but from experience he knew it might take some time to reassure her. The days of the workhouse had left terrible scars on the mind of this poor little soul and his heart bled for her but his mind angered at the man responsible.

Once out of earshot, Aunt Fee could not contain her curiosity, "Izzy!! Who is Izzy, my dear?" holding on to Louise's arm in total confusion. "Mr. Woolmer is accompanied by his young niece Aunt Fee: She is staying in my old room."

Aunt Fee was instantly incandescent on the assumption that she had been 'duped'. "His niece indeed!! I do not think so!! How very unlikely! Is this man married, Louise?" Then, as though she had just thought of something even worse, "Is this a love child, Louise?" She frantically sought out her fan again and rapidly tried to cool her redness. "And I thought what a nice young man he was and here we are with a child. Disgusting!" Louise did her best to refute all these accusations but there was not a second's space in which to interject this onslaught of imaginary conclusions and her negations were not heard. "Why would a grown man go running after a child who has had a bad dream – tell her to shut up and go back to sleep, is what I say. How ridiculous!!" Louise again tried to explain but Aunt Fee fussed on. "I'm so disappointed in you Louise, that you should be cavorting with such a man! What would your mother say?" She took out a lace handkerchief and dabbed her eyes to rid the dry tears. That was the last straw for Louise.

"Aunt Fee!" She suddenly said firmly, arresting the ridiculous diatribe. Calmer now, "Aunt Fee, please do not distress yourself. Mr. Woolmer is a fine young man. He is not married. He is a good and kind guardian of a young child who has suffered considerable trauma and they are welcome in my home. We are not 'cavorting' as you put it and for the record, I believe my dearest mamma would find him inspirational. Now please, can we continue with our meal, which my servants have worked hard to provide for your enjoyment."

Silence reigned awkwardly. Aunt Fee adjusted her bodice indignantly and asked Elders to replenish her glass – full.

Outside, Thunder cursed the cold as he waited patiently in the undergrowth, peering in to the luxurious domestic scene and he had not missed Tobias's exit. Louise was slightly more vulnerable now but he was still not confident enough to move into action.

From the frost-crisp garden, Purrcillus the household tortoiseshell feline pet, observed the amber glowing scene as she approached, soft pawed, towards the rear, mullioned windows of Bancroft House. Hesitating for a single moment, Purrcillus made a sudden leap and landed with silent precision on the wide, stone window sill which was to guide her up to her familiar, elevated external view of the room. Her nose pressed momentarily against the cold glass before she looked upwards towards her next aim and with a perfect, acrobatic pounce, she made a seemingly effortless leap to land softly on the familiar frame of the open transom window above. Without a suggestion of a wobble, she turned gracefully, entranced by the vision of the alluring fireplace within. Aiming for this, her favourite place to curl up for sleep, she made a second launch downwards. Unexpectedly and somewhat unfortunately however, this evening there was a precariously placed candle flickering upon the interior window sill, casting its romantic light across the room. Purrcillus's tail caught it on her descent – and – CLATTER!!

A slight clunk of cutlery on china as Louise and her guests turned simultaneously towards the distraction and in that breath-holding moment, all eyes fell upon the tumbled candle rolling towards the pinned back window drape. Silence fell in that moment of arrested heart beats and then with a sudden WHOOSH, a large flame ignited, flicking upwards like a genie from a lamp. Louise had been standing, mid-motion passing a plate of delightfully creamy dessert to Uncle Gerald. Her eyes averted, in that same moment, it dropped uncontrollably from her hand, rolled across the table and landed in Aunt Fee's beautifully gowned lap. Ignoring her cry of horror, Louise grabbed the carafe of water from the table and moved in what felt like dreamy slow motion towards the window, screeching an involuntary 'NOOOOO!'... As she jettisoned the contents of the carafe towards the flame, the growing flame spattered and did its best to fight back like an angry dragon but for a moment the onslaught of water was just too much and it began to recede.

Uncle Gerald, however, in a fumbling drunken stupour, too left his seat, grabbing onto his generously refilled goblet of treasured Cognac and stumbled forwards. With a grand gesture of finality, as though stabbing his sword through the heart of a beast to defeat it, he hurled the contents of his glass towards the dying flame. With horror, there was a communal gasp as the flame re-ignited with the powerful alcoholic splash.

"Oh dear! I seem to have made it worse!!" Uncle Gerald said, not seeming to quite comprehend the seriousness of his thoughtless action. The flames licked higher and quite quickly, smoke began to permeate the air.

Somewhere in the back of Louise's consciousness, she was suddenly aware of panic behind her. Turning, her focus fell upon Aunt Fee wedged in her chair, directly to the side of the disastrous palaver unfolding. Gasping for breath, Aunt Fee's podgy face had now paled a shade of blue and her eyes bulged wide open as she struggled to drag in oxygen through the now smoke filled atmosphere.

"Get out of the room!!!" screeched Louise to her guests, gesturing wildly. Her urgency was short of panic and she was too well aware of her diminishing control of the situation.

"We need more help!!" She opened the door and screeched loudly, "Jake... Elders... - Come quickly!! Get this fire out!!"

At that same moment, hearing the commotion all the way to the kitchen, Rose's shocked face appeared in the middle of the pandemonium. She immediately turned on her heels and ran back out shouting to the top of her voice for help!

Quickly trying to usher Uncle Gerald out of danger's way, Louise tried to hurriedly guide him staggering in his inebriated state towards the door. Louise's eyes flew wide open as she anticipated further disaster, realizing Violet and Elders were simultaneously bustling urgently towards them from the opposite direction. With no idea how, Uncle Gerald managed to recover his equilibrium enough to exit the room safely. With a random backward glance, Louise could not believe that he had incredulously managed to grab the bottle of cognac on the way. Violet and Elders rushed to the aid of Aunt Fee, trying to cajole her out of her chair. Her coughing fit however, had not subsided and she had no ability to stand up unaided. As large a lady as she was, it was impossible to manoeuvre her heavy weight from the chair and so she remained rigid, static and in increasing peril!!

With brief discussion and miming gestures, Violet and Elders grabbed the back of her chair, tilted her backwards and dragged her as best as they could towards the door, hindered somewhat by her instinctive resistance and flailing arms.

Jake, ran into the room to witness wild panic, drew up another chair beside the window and against Louise's remonstrations, leapt upon it and snatched at the burning fabric from above, pulling its heavy weight downwards. The action was successful in bringing to the ground the entire window dressing and as it fell to the floor its density fortuitously dampened the fire's spirit and a darkness fell upon the room as the flame died. Regrettably, in doing so, the impetuosity of such efforts propelled him backwards. The chair on which he stood teetered and rocked. Impossible to keep his balance, he tumbled heavily rearwards and fell disastrously into the side of the glazed display cupboard behind him.

All of Louise's mother's treasured possessions proudly displayed within responded with a sickening crash.

Tobias, hearing the screeches and clatter, came rushing into the room all too late, to see nothing short of carnage.

Thunder witnessed the whole epic disaster. Knowing now that his chances of kidnapping Louise were well and truly scuppered, he dreaded returning to Mr. Partridge again without the Lady but also with the news that his neighbour's house had caught fire!

Chapter 21

Christmas Eve had finally come and Louise woke to the comfortable realization that at least Aunt Fee and Uncle Gerald would be leaving today. It seemed like the smoke had permeated the entire house but Louise told herself that this was probably her own exaggeration, although the wheezing Aunt Fee complained the entire time about the malodour and her incapacity to breathe. Neither could Aunt Fee find it in herself to look at Mr. Woolmer, even when he addressed her directly. Gone was the high pedestal she had put him upon when they met. In her eyes he was now persona non grata, which Louise and Tobias both thought rather amusing.

The staff had been wonderful in clearing away the horror of last evening's fiasco. Tobias too had taken the lead on suggesting how Louise might go forward with resurrecting the room and she was so glad to have him there to assist and advise. There was less damage to items in the display cabinet than first imagined, although Louise had no idea how. She was still able to salvage most, which relieved her conscience immensely.

Izzy was much improved but they had encouraged her to have one more day in 'her' bedroom to keep her out of harms way whilst the work was going on and keep her safe from the soot and stench, which would have aggravated her chest. She did not need any incentive to stay put and played happily with the books and toys on loan from Louise. In a quiet moment, popping in to her room, Louise had suggested that Izzy draw a picture to leave for Father Christmas, should he call by this evening. So with a few coloured chalks and piece of slate, she left an excited little girl sitting up in bed, deciding what to draw.

By early afternoon, the dining room was cleared of its major collateral damage and everywhere was cleaned. The windows were left open, despite the cold air but with the door firmly closed, the draught was largely excluded.

At least, the Christmas tree still stood in the salon, so all was not lost.

By next morning, Thunder needed to use the water closet at least three times before he dared report to Mr. Partridge. He was certain of another beating, or worse that Mr. Partridge would again bundle him off to the workhouse where he had rescued him from and place him in the worst of sections. He could not bear that! He had one choice only and that was to face him. He was sure his next night would be spent at that dreaded place but then he was beginning to think that the better alternative might be, to be buried in the woods with the others.

No choice, he thought to himself and took a deep breath! He knocked on the library door and heard the familiar "Come!" Resisting the thought of the water closet one more time, he entered the room, eyes downwards. "Well??" questioned Mr. Partridge.

"Sir, I went to the Lady's 'ouse, Sir... but see there was a fire and..."

"And what, you blithering idiot?"

"Well Sir, I cudnt get her Sir."

Standing now, Mr. Partridge shouted, "What the hell do you mean they had a fire so you couldn't get her? - We all have fires you imbecile. Have you not seen them?" He gestured towards the grate, impatiently.

Rushing his words, "No Sir... I mean, like a big fire, like up the 'ouse Sir. Flames like reachin' the sky!!"

"Oh! Did they now?!!!" He thought for a moment. "How bad? Whereabouts?"

"Whur them served the food, posh like. Thur woz lots of people there too Sir and an ol' fella he was very 'arf, 'arf an arf he wus!" Thunder felt the need to demonstrate a drunkard. Then thur was a big crash and stuff fell over and folk were coffin'."

"Well that just might have saved you Thunder!" Thunder had no idea what he was talking about but the words seemed to be good.

With a rare spurious smile, Mr. Partridge continued, "This is good news, Thunder!! They have guests. It is the festive season and they have no dining hall. Excellent!" Sitting at his bureau, he scrawled a flamboyant script, threw a generous amount of chalk to dry the ink and folded the parchment and thumped upon it his seal.... Thunder I need you to take a message. You can also go to the workhouse and tell Smythe I shall not be there today."

It had been lashing it down with rain mixed in with sleet and occasionally hailstones, since early morning. The frosts and seasonal weather had for the moment gone and been replaced by dreary, damp, cold darkness. The windows in the outside laundry room were steamed up with condensation from the small mountain of linens, which had accumulated over the past few days. It would all take an age to dry in such winter weather and the house fire incident had left the table linen permeated with the stench of smoke and they would be needed again for the night after tomorrow, as the household was short on supplies of full-length table linen. Everything had to be turned around as quickly as possible and the sooner the better the washing was done, so that the task of drying could begin.

Betsy was not best pleased to have all this extra work to do, on top of her routine expectations but with a certain amount of grumbling, she tried to delegate as much as possible to her new assistants and aspired to the unrealistic challenge that lay before her for fear of letting down her Ladyship. Her own role had escalated and now extended to being in charge of and training two young maids.

Rose and Violet were instructed in the order of things and set to work as early as the daylight would allow. However, the rain clouds were so low and heavy that they held back any real chance of full daylight for most of the day, making life even harder for the young maids inspecting the stains on what should be crisp white linen.

Heating as much water as they could, to boil out some of the worst stained items, at least brought some feeling of warmth into the room. 'Room', to be honest, was a rather grand word. Perhaps barn would have been a more appropriate term for this outhouse. When Louise had first arrived at Bancroft House, it was as if she was viewing it for the first time, with fresh eyes, since she was now 'in charge' of the running of the home. One of Louise's first priorities, she decided, had been to improve the laundry facilities, as it was surely time to upgrade. It was just a matter of waiting for such inclement winter weather as they were currently experiencing to pass, before they set to on rebuilding and extending the building to incorporate a fire and some newer 'equipment'. In the meantime, she fully appreciated the difficulties the maids were under and hated to see how their weary bodies struggled with the cold, damp working conditions. Hauling the heavy, wet fabrics up high onto drying racks was arduous work and she hated to see how their hands almost bled with chilblains from the extremes of demands upon them. Work to improve matters would begin as soon as she could arrange it.

Rose and Violet had been working as best as they could but had not made much progress over the morning. A few hours into their tasks, just as Rose had lifted the latest of the saturated bed linens onto one of the drying racks, it collapsed under the weight of wet bedding. It had been promising to collapse during use over the past few weeks but they had continued to use it on a wing and a prayer. The girls let out a screech as it fell to the ground and onto the dusty floor, enforcing a secondary wash. Each girl blamed the other for not taking a broom to the floor first as they had been taught to do... but it was too late now and futile to argue. They each eventually fell silent in their own annoyance and simply carried on.

The mishap did however, put back their progress and their hard work had been wasted. Such a push back in time was indeed unfortunate. They dreaded Betsy coming over to check their progress, as she surely would not be impressed! They really did not want to get the rough end of her tongue and hated to think what sort of punishment they may face. No lunch would be bad enough but continuing without a break at all, until all tasks were finished, was quite another dread! At this rate they could be working by candlelight until supper time. They didn't even feel they had time enough to leave the laundry to fetch Jake to come and fix the airer. They would do as much as they could first before that task became a priority.

Rain continued to torrent and the sound on the impoverished roof was almost deafening. At times they had to almost shout in order to communicate. Under usual circumstances, they would chat idly about whatever gossip came to their heads but not today. Today was hard.

Once the tablecloths had been washed in the huge tubs, they each took an end and twisted the cloth between them until the twirl of fabric met in the middle like a rope. Tightly they squeezed until as much water drained from each one as possible. It gave the desired effect of promoting drying but on a day like today, this had to be done inside and consequently the floor of the laundry area became as wet as outside.

Violet cursed her inadequate shoes. Her left foot was

completely soaked now and she could barely keep on her shoe, with its sole hanging half off. She could hardly feel her toes at all and as she moved about the place, she often tripped. Rose chastised her for not getting it mended sooner but Violet just looked embarrassed, not wanting to explain it was not due to inattentiveness, so much as inability to pay a cobbler. Coming from the poorest of the poor families, she had desperately needed this job and as soon as she could, she would be able to purchase some essentials for herself, send some money home to her mother and hopefully put some coins by so as never to be that poor again. Repaired shoes would be a priority.

Sometime after midday, during a lull in the heavy showers, they recognised the dreaded splash of footsteps through the muddy puddles between the house and the laundry. Their stomachs churned with apprehension. Keeping their eyes firmly lowered downwards towards their job in hand, they tried to avoid a glance up, as Betsy pushed her way in through the semi collapsed quirky door, which needed lifting by the latch and forcing open with a shoulder in order to enter. The damp weather had made the wood even more cantankerous and Betsy growled at it in annoyance. Her mood was not enhanced as she stepped inside and slipped upon the internal saturated floor. Fortunately, she regained her balance but then her eyes scanned the room in disbelief. An audible gasp fled from her lips.

Looking at the broken rack, half suspended from the ceiling and splintered across the floor, then glancing back towards the girls, her reaction was not at all what they had anticipated.

"Please tell me you didn't have clean linens on there when it broke??"

"Yes, Miss Tyler" they chorused, both becoming crimson cheeked, waiting for the expected scolding.

Huffing out aloud Betsy continued, "Argh how annoying! It's been waiting to do this since we arrived but WHY would it choose today to break!!! So much to do!! How much have you had to re-wash? Please tell me you DID rewash??"

"Yes Miss Tyler." said Violet braving a response. "There was a good deal to start again, so we are doing our best. Sorry Miss Tyler but we are really behind ourselves now. We didn't like to spare the time to even get Jake to fix it Miss Tyler. Should I go now Miss Tyler??" Apologies kept tumbling from her mouth.

Almost patiently, Betsy said they should continue in the laundry room and she herself would go fetch Jake. With that, muttering words of incredulity beneath her breath, she splatted her feet through the inside puddles and onto the mud outside.

Releasing their breath, Rose and Violet let out a huge sigh of relief as the door was hauled to behind Betsy. "Don't know how we got away with that!" said Violet turning towards Rose. Rose looked white. "Me neither!" confirmed Rose.

Just then, the door was manoeuvered open again. In stepped Jake. "I've just passed Miss Tyler. She said I had to fix this here rack … What have you done to it??" Before the girls could answer, he added, "Oh and she said you had to go do an errand for her Rose… You'd best go now!"

Violet's heart thumped in her chest. She was secretly pleased she would be alone with Jake at last for a while and flashed him a shy smile through bright pink cheeks then dropped her eyes again towards her work. Rose, on the other hand was gratified for the release from her chores and quickly dried her sore hands on her damp apron before setting off through the temperamental doorway. Curiosity, however, soon crossed her mind as to what chore lay ahead. Dipping her head against the rain, she skipped lightfoot across the mud towards the back door of the house in the hope of not getting too muddy and reveled in the instant warmth of the kitchen fire as she came through the back door.

Hopeful that the chore Miss Tyler had in mind would be indoors, she called out to announce her arrival as she made her way past the pantry down two steps into the kitchen. She slipped off her damp apron and hung it over the back of a chair in front of the fire and almost immediately watched the steam rise from it as it began to dry. She wrung her hands and held them out in front of the red blaze then repeated the action.

Betsy looked up from the baking table. She was surrounded by an array of ingredients and the kitchen smelled wonderful. Rose's stomach gurgled in response to the idea of warm buns cooking in the oven. She suddenly realized how hungry she was! It was so cosy in here with the fire stoked with fragrant logs, freshly baked cakes and the sound of the rain thrashing against the leaded windows. Her toes and fingers tingled now as the warmth began to permeate her body. This soon turned to pain and she grimaced against the now familiar discomfort as the blood coursed back into her fingertips. She held her hands under her armpits and walked around the room to distract herself from the agony. It would soon pass... well eventually.

Betsy spoke. Make yourself a jar of hot milk she said kindly. Perhaps Miss Tyler wasn't so fearsome after all, Rose mused. "Here" she nodded to a bowl, "Put a bit of this nutmeg in to taste." Rose was aghast at her kindness and responded with profuse thanks and a gratifying smile.

Feeling better now and only too pleased to be back in the warmth, Rose actually looked forward to a chore in here and wondered what it was that Miss Tyler had in mind for her to help with.

"Right girl!" Started Betsy, 'Get your coat on, I need you to go into the village for me!"

Horrified, Rose looked at Betsy with utter disbelief.

Violet took advantage of the rare opportunity to have a heart to heart with Jake. She found it difficult to approach the subject of his recent and reluctant confession but this was the ideal moment whilst they were alone. She had no intention of forgetting what he had confided in her, although Jake really would have preferred to leave the subject in the past where they left it.

Violet, to her credit, had a wonderful quality of employing a gently persuasive manner and it was ultimately not difficult for Jake to disclose his secret. He was embarrassed to divulge how he had been bullied and even more mortified to reveal his association with a murder. She listened with compassion and understanding and felt a sense of pride that he had been able to share his fears and misdeeds with Lady Louise. She would know what to do!

A note arrived for Tobias from his own solicitor by private messenger. The two men had studied together and trusted each other with their lives. The message had been sent on from his home address to Bancroft House by dint of its urgency. Tobias had hoped it would find its way there. It was the response to his enquiry some days ago, even though then he had not expected to be still there at Bancroft House.

The feedback to Tobias's suspicions and questions was very illuminating. His friend had been able to find for Tobias a reputable private detective as requested, to carry out some investigations in Childswickham village. Thus far, they were able to confirm, that there had indeed been a previous detective, who had been assigned to the task of investigating Mr. Partridge. He had been employed by a Mr. Smythe, a co-founder of Broadside Workhouse. Unfortunately, this agent had mysteriously gone missing after a very short time. The man's brief was in response to Smythe becoming concerned about a dubious number of suspicious disappearances from the workforce at Broadside... they had all been women.

Just as worrying, there had been an influx of workers who had been coerced to leave their jobs and forced to serve time in the workhouse. They were not there because they had been unemployed or were homeless or even in poverty ... they were there because they had been blackmailed. All information pointed to Mr. Partridge. An augmented workforce meant more profit for greedy founders of the workhouse. Smythe however, on discovering something despicable was afoot, was disturbed by such dubiosity. Smythe prided himself on being a more empathetic owner and wanted to keep the distinction between workhouse and prison. He was most certainly not a criminal and did not wish to be embroiled in filthy reputation.

There was one particular incident, which brought a red flag to Smythe's attention and led to his further enquiries. A young girl presented one day at the entrance of the workhouse, in great distress and in floods of tears, begging to be heard... there was an agitated desperateness about her that was different from the rest. Most came with a resigned sense of hopelessness. There would be an almost tangible deep depression hanging over them to be arriving at these doors with emaciated families and a dread of being separated as they clung to each other. Once within the walls, they were parted, sent to be stripped and scoured clean, they feared that they might never see each other again. Some did not. Others were punished hard if found communicating with each other. They grieved for each other, deeply feared for their future, for their loved ones, for their sanity and even for their lives. This was never a place to come without it being a very last resort.

Yet this girl came in search of someone. She was screaming in desperation and not really making sense. Amongst the hullaballoo, Smythe had initially suspected her rage was due to being 'mad as hops' and just one of some in society who had lost their capable thought. She was claiming her sister had been stolen and been falsely imprisoned there. It all seemed highly dramatic and rather unlikely to Smythe, yet her insistence raged in a way that Smythe's attention was gripped and there was something about her that he almost believed.

Despite her tiny frame, the supervisors had been taken aback and were struggling to restrain her but suddenly she flew into an even greater frenzy on seeing Thunder pass by, having collected his wages from the office. With instant recognition she propelled herself with such force she broke free from those restraining her, shouting "It's him!!!" The supervisors caught up with her grabbing her arms behind her and pulled her to the floor. "He did it, don't you hear me?!! He took her and ..." Thrusting her finger towards Thunder she bawled at him, "You took her!! I saw you ... filthy beast you are" she spat at the ground " ...I saw you ...she was screaming to let her go and you still took her..."

Thunder laughed in her face as she squirmed on the dirt floor. "Shut up y'old bag. Get 'er out of 'ere" he told the supervisors.

"I saw you ...you took her against that tree and pressed yourself against her I SAW YOU! She fought with you but you did those things to her...You locked me in ... I couldn't help her... It was you....I saw what you did ...YOU RAPED HER!!! ...She is but a child!!!" Overwhelmed with grief and distress, she could barely breathe as she screamed these last words.

"Ha!! I wuz lettin' off steam!! Shut up and get 'er out of 'ere!"

The girl crumbled, expired of energy... and sobbed. The staff began to haul her towards the door. The movement rallied her a little, "Where is she? Where did you take her?? Is she here? Please let her go ... PLEASE let her go....", she sobbed bitterly.

Struggling against them now and shouting over her shoulder to the smirking monster, "She's just a child... she's my baby sister. Please tell me where she is" Screaming her plea and in absolute desperation she added, 'Please ...take me instead... TAKE ME!!! LET HER GO!!!"...

"STOP!" Smythe stepped forward, angrily. He had been heading in the opposite direction when the kerfuffle began. Slowly engrossed in the erupting scene, he gradually retraced his steps and observed the drama. "What in God's name is all this about?" He looked towards Thunder for an explanation.

Thunder froze with fear. Now what did he say? If he told the truth that he was being blackmailed by Mr. Partridge to bring in extra workers for his 'pleasure', he doubted he would be believed. If he refuted the allegations; now that might be the best way – it was his word against hers. Yet he knew how bad he was at lying... if he got found out for all he'd done, he'd be back in the workhouse as an inmate anyway. Or worse still, prison.

"Well?" Thunder jolted back to the moment under Smythe's prompt.

"Er well Sir, I don't know wot she's talkin' about, Sir"

"Yes you do!!!" "Don't lie!!! What is going on here?" He looked towards the girl, still half lying on the filthy floor and their eyes connected, hers pleading through the tears. He wondered if it was because in some way, that glance of the eye reminded him of his own daughter but he felt a strange sense of responsibility for this young woman.

Ignoring Thunder's mute response, he commanded the supervisors let go of the girl and with that she slowly stood, her knees grazed and bleeding from the dragging.

"Tell me your story, girl" he bid her more gently.

The girl cried her way through the tragedy she had witnessed and how she had come to find her beloved sister. Thunder huffed and puffed throughout her words.

"Is what she is saying your truth too Thunder?" Thunder dropped his eyes but still pleaded certain innocence, "Just like I say, Sir, lettin' off some steam."

"Get upstairs to my office immediately!"

Thunder did not move, more from fear of losing bladder control than anything else. "I said NOW!!" Smythe's heels physically left the floor as he shouted.

Turning to the staff, he instructed them to stay with the girl but not to touch her or speak. "I shall return shortly!" Without further word, his direct gaze into the girl's eyes was, to her, somehow reassuring. He then added, "I am sorry."

She was astonished by this unexpected kindness.

He set off up the stairs and slammed the door behind him once in the office with Thunder. A berating rant lasted some time until Thunder finally emerged, holding his hands in front of his wet pants.

Smythe had needed to understand why in the first place, Thunder was involved in abducting this young girl, if that were true! He was also aware that for whatever reason, Partridge had withdrawn this man from the workhouse by way of some cock and bull story about needing extra help at his mansion. Thunder was however, periodically still seen walking the floors of the building, with one excuse or another. Now that Smythe came to consider it, it was rather odd. He had no difficulty in grinding down Thunder to tell him all about his relationship with Partridge and the work that he found himself instructed to do. Despite his giant like exterior, he was a very nervous and scared man who was clearly being blackmailed by Partridge, although Thunder did not even seem to understand that that was the case, just that he was terrified of him.

Whilst Thunder gave Smythe the gist of being dog's body and described some of the tasks he was forced to do, under threat of being returned to the workhouse or sent to prison, including abducting young women, he did not go so far as to admit he had disposed of three victims at the behest of his master, plus he had himself killed one other by misfortune, in the woods.

Smythe began to consider his co-founder Mr. Partridge, in a different light. He had begun to uncover more than he was expecting and his suspicions about his colleague were seemingly worse than he could ever have imagined. It seemed that Mr. Partridge was suspected of being involved in considerable duplicity and was known for violence and coercive behaviour, most unbecoming of his position as a senior administrator. Smythe had no intention of becoming tarred with the same brush. This matter needed to be dealt with officially.

Chapter 22

Tobias, by return of post, gave further instruction to continue investigations. He offered as much further information or suspicions as possible and urged the detectives to make their way to the vicinity as quickly as possible to get to the truth.

The kitchen was a hub of activity preparing for a feast the next day. They may well now be without a dining room but Louise had organized the staff to improvise and transform the parlour into a make-do dining area. They astonished her with their creativity and the room looked festive and inviting.

Louise was rather excited that her father would be there to join them, arriving at the very latest, Christmas morning and Aunt Fee and uncle Gerald would by then have left to continue their journey north in time for the festivities. Just as she was reveling in her plans for the next day, Elders brought a silver tray to Louise and she took the note from it with curiosity. Opening the seal, her heart sank as she brought an anxious hand to her face. Aunt Fee drew breath from her current monologue to enquire after her wellbeing.

"It is a note from Mr. Partridge... our next door neighbour." Tobias raised his head with concern. Louise scanned the letter and in précis of its content, said, "He's inviting us all for dinner, this evening." She looked at Tobias, "I don't really want to go."

"Don't be ridiculous, child," Aunt Fee thought her opinion was valuable. "When you say neighbour, you do not mean the

exquisite mansion we drove past on our way here, do you?....
the one set upon the hillside with the sweeping drive?" With
excitement, she managed to elevate herself out of her chair with
inordinate ease and took a step towards Louise, snatching the
invitation from her hand to read it herself. Louise nodded. "Oh
for Pete's sake child, of course you must go!!" We shall go too
– the invitation says clearly 'all guests'. It would be too rude not
to go. Is this man married?" She wondered out aloud. Without
reason, she added, "I doubt it!! I suppose he's extremely debonair
- this sort of man usually is ...it's time we looked for a husband
for you Louise. She glanced a dismissive glare at Tobias. Since
your dear Mamma is no longer with us, I shall be happy to take
on this role. I expect he is terribly wealthy... I imagine he is most
influential, knows a lot of important people. Mr. Woolmer, of
course, will NOT be able to go" emphasizing the negative, "..
He will stay here with his daughter – or niece or whatever ...
and for propriety's sake you cannot go alone. You must have a
chaperone. Oh how exciting! I shall go and find which gown
is most suitable for me to wear. Please send up Violet, Louise.
I shall need her to attend to me..." and as she was making to
exit the room, wheezing through her words, she continued over
her shoulder, "and Louise do make sure you dress your hair
respectfully: None of this 'a la mode' paraphernalia. Send a
message to our driver – we shall delay our travel until tomorrow
morning!" With that, she left the room with surprising agility.

Tobias and Louise looked at each other in disbelief.

"I am so sorry for her rudeness, Tobias!" She then added,
"Tobias, you will come too won't you? Please?"....

Holding his hand out to take hers, "No." He smiled gently.
"Your aunt is right, Louise, I cannot leave Izzy here and
especially not on Christmas Eve. There is every chance she will
wake early to see if Father Christmas has already arrived and
you know how she cannot settle knowing I am not here." He hid

his concerns and continued, "I know where you are and your safety is assured in the company of Aunt Fee and Uncle Gerald. They will act as your protection. It will look more suspicious that we are on to him if you do not go. You can feign an early exit due to Aunt Fee's morning departure. Do not worry. I shall not retire until you are safely back home. I shall stay here and await your father's arrival. I feel sure he will manage to get here today."

Louise smiled feeling a little more reassured, and left the room to prepare for the dreaded evening.

Rose's father had not visited in a while and Rose's wages had been accumulating in the meantime. Louise suspected that the bad weather had hindered his visitation, although that surprised her a great deal. Rose on the other hand, believed it more likely to be as a result of him getting drunk and incapable of the walk, despite the promise of money and even though it was not too great a distance.

Secretly, Rose hoped that her father might turn up trumps and arrive with a small Christmas gift for her, although he had never done so before and she realized this was never really likely to happen.

She could only ever remember once receiving a gift. It was from her mother on her deathbed. She lovingly pressed into her hand a small, flimsy chain upon which hung a pendant with a lock of hair, belonging to her own mother and her mother closed Rose's fingers around it in the hope that she would keep it safe. It was gifted as a treasured piece and the only thing that that she had to offer her daughter as a token of her love. Rose had ever since cherished it but it was so very precious to her but since the chain was fragile, she never wore it for fear of losing it and kept it lovingly wrapped in her mother's only embroidered handkerchief which was furtively tucked away in a small tapestry travel bag under her bed. From time to time, she would take it out of its hiding place, simply to hold in her hands for just moments and think of her mother, the act of which seemed to restore her spiritual connection with her mother and make her feel once again, that she was loved.

By the time Rose reached Broadway village, she could barely feel her hands or feet again. The rain was no longer quite so incessant but the showers were sharp when they came. She was uncomfortably soaked. The excitement of Christmas Eve had been diluted as they endeavoured to achieve all their chores. There still remained a mountain of work to achieve before Christmas morning and Rose's thoughts encircled her in a dreamlike state. Happy recollections, mixed with chores to do, spun around in her jumbled head. She was always thus! A mismatch of thoughts going on at the same time like a kaleidoscope. People called her scatterbrain and her nickname at home was Dizzy. She was often chided as being so silly or even stupid. She was used to it!

Amongst this whirr of thoughts, she flicked her head suddenly to look behind her responding to a noise somewhere perhaps in the bushes. She felt her heart bump a beat. She stopped momentarily but nothing stirred. She continued on her way, assuming it was probably a deer or fox in the undergrowth. Nevertheless, she was strangely reassured by the sight of the roof of the Posting House above the tree-lined lane and she sped up her steps.

Her clothes now heavy and dripping with icy water, she just put her mind to her instruction of errands. Exiting the Bindery where she had been instructed to collect a repaired book for Lady Louise, she now concentrated on the kitchen checklist. Betsy had especially needed cloves, chestnuts, arrowroot and a bottle of best cognac, as the next delivery to the house was still days away. These were neatly packaged up and in her shopping basket. Remembering her last errand at the Posting House, she decided she would first cross the road to look in her favourite shop window, the haberdashers. Distracted with this thought, she stepped into the road. A horse and cart sped by, narrowly missing her, splashing her from the waist down in slimy, muddy, ice-cold filth. The driver swore vehemently as he hauled the horses around her to avoid running her down altogether. Amongst other words – he called her stupid!!!

Reflecting on this as she shyly exchanged essential dialogue with the postmaster, she found herself wondering – 'Why WAS she so stupid?' She didn't mean to be, she mused. She supposed she was just always thinking of something else! She had to admit to herself though, that things did just seem to happen to her. She hated being stupid. It was a moment of awakening for Rose and she resolved in that moment: "Right, from now on," she promised herself, "She would not be stupid any longer!!!"

Errands completed, Rose picked up her steps and headed back towards the house, imagining the warmth of the kitchen and that welcoming fire. She pushed her free hand into her wet pocket as though to keep her warmer and steadying her shopping basket, turned the corner at the end house to follow the pathway back.

A woman screeched out from behind, "Cum back 'here you little thieving beggar!!" As Rose turned towards the hullaballoo she was hit head on by a scraggy urchin of a lad. The pair spun like a whirlwind but as he slipped away and escaped like a wiry fox, Rose lost her footing and landed with a crack on the floor and a simultaneous smash of glass. She looked down with horror at her cognac soaked skirt...

It had been a long and difficult journey for Lord Dorchester. He knew that Louise would be expecting him in time for Christmas Day, as the roads were now rid of snow and ice but the harsh winter rain had now set in and the horses were slipping as they dragged the carriage through the muddy roads.

They had set off early morning the day before but they had barely reached Witney when they hit a deep pothole creating a resounding 'snap'. Fortunately, Lord Dorchester's driver Jimmy, was sufficiently experienced to be able to calmly bring the horses to an immediate halt, realizing the axle had probably snapped and put a wheel out of kilter. He had anticipated the incident with fast reaction, managing to avert a terrible accident, however it did mean that he needed to make an on the spot temporary repair in order to get them to safety but the carriage would not be safe enough to go much further. They would need to make an overnight stay somewhere in Witney. Once back on the road, they were at least able to slowly roll along until they found an inn, which offered less than reputable overnight accommodation.

Morning came after a restless night and Lord Dorchester was keen to get on his way again. Frustratingly, the axle was still only poorly remedied, as a replacement was not available. Thus, they set off slowly and needing to drive with great caution. It had been secured as best as could be done to get them back on the road but the onward journey was therefore slow, arduous and an anxious time for both driver and passenger. Eventually, they approached Fish Hill and Bancroft House was a short distance away. Light was fading fast.

Approaching the house along the rough drive, which led only to the house, the driver slowed to precariously avoid a young girl sitting on the edge of the roadway. Slowly navigating the carriage around her, Lord Dorchester glanced through the window and also saw the girl and realized she was crying. He banged on the roof of the carriage as instruction for the driver to halt.

Rose had dared not return to Bancroft House for fear of punishment. Instead, she sat shaking on a ridge of wet mud, sobbing. Her brandy drenched skirts hung from her thighs.

Her mind was in the depths of despair. She barely noticed the gentleman approaching on foot.

Louise came down the stairs to meet Tobias's eyes. She took his breath away... "Louise" he paused, "You look beautiful." She cast her eyes downwards, just for a brief moment to revel in his compliment, before smiling her appreciation and he noticed how her left cheek dimpled. "I very much wish you were escorting me there" she replied sincerely." "As do I," he returned, "More than you know!" He took her hand as though to assist her from the lowest stair and clasped his other hand around it. "Perhaps one evening you will allow me to do so, for I would be honoured to have you take my arm to attend a resplendent occasion." Louise flushed a deep red and smiled a beguiling smile, "I shall await your invitation, Sir." adding an elegantly flirtatious curtsy.

Aunt Fee broke the spell of the moment with her wheezy interruption as she shouted enticement for her husband to be quicker in his step. The carriage arrived and they departed, leaving Tobias wondering if after all, he ought to have dissuaded Louise from going

As the carriage pulled away, Tobias immediately felt the loss of Louise's company and instinctively felt the need to see Izzy. He peeped soundlessly around the door of her room, to find her curled up amongst the bed linen, breathing softly, fast asleep. He studied her beautiful face, as he often did, seeking the likeness of his dear sister with her long eyelashes resting closed against her cheeks and a curled forelock of hair across her temple.

She was such a sweetheart – a heart breaker. How could he ever have thought he could give her up? His dialogue with Lord Dorchester had been so convincing that it seemed completely the right decision for Louise to take guardianship of Izzy but he had no idea why her father had made no mention of this to his daughter before he arrived. There was no doubt at all in Tobias's mind, that Louise would make a perfect guardian. She would be loving, caring, inspirational and as devoted as any mother could be. What was more, Izzy was clearly growing to love her. Perhaps he was too. The thought flew through his mind like an arrow. A sudden and honest realization hit him. His heart seemed to stop.

Chapter 23

Tobias sat next to his niece's bed for some time – he had no idea how long, musing over his latest revelation. Bouncer, taking up what had become his habitual place, yawned at the foot of the bed and shifted his position. As Tobias, moved his gaze towards the dog, he caught sight of Izzy's slate, left for Father Christmas at the side of her bed. He picked it up to decipher the picture she had drawn. She had chalked her child's image of a man and a woman holding hands and the woman wore a bridal dress and veil. Next to them was a little girl. Each person was labelled, Uncle Tobias, Lady Louise, Izzy. The title read 'Please, Father Christmas.'

Just then Tobias heard voices downstairs. He recognized that of Louise's father and descended the staircase with alacrity to welcome him. Lord Dorchester was taken aback to find Tobias still there but hid his surprise well. They greeted each other with fond respect and Tobias asked Elders to serve food immediately as he felt sure his late arrival must mean he would be hungry.

The moment that Louise set eyes upon her host, her dislike for him intensified. He greeted his three evening guests with extreme charm and Aunt Fee was enthralled by the ostentatious welcome, enormous house and perhaps even more so by the apparent wealth of their host. As they stepped out of the carriage, she was still giving Louise instruction on how to act alluringly and throughout the introductions, she persisted in pushing Louise forward, gesturing how to act and move. Already, Louise could not wait to go home!

Mr. Partridge was possibly almost as old as her father and had about him a certain manner, which made Louise's skin crawl. He was overweight and as the evening progressed, he began to sweat profusely. His odour was unpleasant and he salivated excessively when he spoke. Once the meal began, it became apparent that he over imbibed and as he did so, his wig slipped. Louise could barely take her eyes off it, as it came perilously close to slipping off altogether, before he persisted in raking it back, more or less into place. She found him grotesque and repulsive.

The meal was extravagant as was the quantity of alcohol. Louise had realized early on, that if she did not drink, he could not refill her glass. The tactic worked quite well and it seemed that she was the only one in the room who remained within her senses.

Conversation was boring although Aunt Fee seemed to lap up everything Mr. Partridge had to say and she was beginning to be irritated by her over loud, false wheezy laugh. Louise did not want, nor even need to contribute to the dialogue since Aunt Fee and their host had it covered between them. Louise was by now accustomed to Uncle Gerald mumbling to himself incoherently and completely bypassing current dialogue, voicing only the occasional irrelevance, which everyone ignored. Her mind just drifted off back to her home and the roaring fire, which awaited her – along with Tobias.

Refusing yet another offer of more wine, her thoughts flashed to Izzy, curled up safely in her bed and then she tried to imagine the place in which Tobias had found her. The thought that this man she was accepting the hospitality of, could be so cruel to those innocent young children, just to provide him with the luxury she sat amidst, brought over a wave of nausea.

"Don't you think so, Louise??... LOUISE!!" Aunt Fee's voice jolted her back to the moment. She immediately excused herself from the table to powder her nose. A maid came to escort her to the appropriate room and left her there. She tried to waste as much time as she could just sitting gazing into the gilded mirror, wishing away her time here in this dishonest house. Eventually, gathering up her velvet reticule, she decided to return to the table with a plan to suggest that they take their leave and return to Bancroft House. She couldn't wait to get home!

With that in mind, Louise pulled herself together and returned to the dining room. En route through the hallway, she saw with relief, Aunt Fee having assistance to put on her cloak ready to leave. "Ah, yes" interrupted Louise keenly, "It is time we left, Mr. Partridge."

Wishing to seem polite, Louise turned to her host, desperate to leave, "Thank you Sir, for your hospitality. If I might also have my cloak, we shall say goodnight, Sir?"

Aunt Fee turned to Louise and tutted away the suggestion. "Oh my dear, no, no!" she dismissed emphatically. "Of course you must stay longer in appreciation of Mr. Partridge's kind invitation!" She used her wide eyes with a negative gesture of her head, to convey that Louise must not contradict her insistence that she must stay. "I must take my leave my dear, so that I may get some rest before our early departure in the morning."

Making towards the arched oak doorway, held open by the butler, Louise's panicked voice, halted her momentarily, "'But Aunt Fee...propriety!" it was the only 'code' she could think of, to prevent Aunt Fee leaving her alone with Mr. Partridge.

"Oh my dear... of course! That is all taken care of – uncle Gerald is remaining with you!" With that, she huffed and wheezed her way out of the door with a final goodnight to Mr. Partridge and accepted assistance into the carriage.

Louise had stopped breathing with trepidation. She spun

on her feet to look towards the dining room with dread, to see uncle Gerald in the armchair next to the fire, fast asleep and snoring with a glass of brandy tilted in his hand spilling its contents onto his trousers."

As the front door closed, Louise felt a hand on her backside with a squeeze and the nausea returned as he ushered her forward to another room. "Let us share some time together pretty lady, I would very much like to get to know you better."

Whilst Tobias and Lord Dorchester enjoyed convivial conversation over dinner, Elders had unpacked his master's belongings and prepared his bedroom for an early night. He had instructed Elders to send to the kitchen the bottle of brandy he had brought with him with the message that Rose had left it by error in the carriage when he brought her home from the village. He winked at Elders in indication not to ask any questions and Elders understood his kindness.

Rose had gone straight to her room to remove her ruined skirt and replace it with her only other remaining one. By the time she had reached the kitchen, a bottle of brandy was on the refectory table adjacent to the goods Betsy had requested. She smiled to herself in grateful thanks to Sir Dorchester. She had never known such kindness and realized the stark contrast with her own father.

"Please do not do that Sir!" Louise implored her host as he slipped his hand across her shoulder.

'Oh, come my dear girl, nothing wrong with a little friendly gesture!"

"Sir, I do not like you touching me. It is not appropriate."

"Quite the little Miss Prim are we not?" he jibed, raising his eyebrows, secretly liking the challenge..

"I should like to go home now please. I shall go to wake my uncle. Please find my shawl", she added firmly. She went to walk away from him towards the door but he threw his arm straight across in front of her, barring her way.

Trying to push past him, he resisted her effort and used his other hand to bring her around to face him. Holding her there facing him, he gripped both his sweating hands around her upper arms and used his thumbs to stroke her breasts.

She shrieked "No!! Let me go!" then shouted loudly for uncle Gerald but knowing he would never hear her. Even if he did, she knew he would be too incapable to help her.

He laughed at her feeble attempts to help herself and tried to bring his face towards hers. She squirmed away from his salivating mouth in disgust and pushed hard against his chest with her wrists. He still held her fast.

"Now, now! Do not be so hasty, pretty lady. I am sure we can have a little fun here – if you understand my meaning... Or perhaps you are playing games with me!!" He threw his head back to laugh at the thought of a little bit of excitement and his wig slipped just a little. "Well if you REALLY want to play games, my dear, I think I should show you something upstairs which will erm... enthral you!!"

Holding her firmly now, he twisted her wrists behind her back so tight she could not free herself at all. He manoeuvred her towards the bottom of the stairs and forced her upwards, step by step. Tripping on her gown, he yanked her back on her feet. She was still screaming for her uncle to wake up but the stinking breath in her ear continued to chide her with promises of disgusting acts awaiting her.

Once at the top of the stairs, he pushed her along the corridor towards a door on the left and kicked the base panel. The door opened onto a highly gilded, ostentatious room. Once inside the room, he fiddled behind him with one hand to turn the large key in the lock, then pushed her forwards, controlling her steps towards a huge four poster bed which dominated the space. He threw her the last few steps onto the mattress. She instinctively tried to scramble to her feet but he was too quick for her and his broad frame blocked her way.

"Do not touch me, you vile man!!" she warned him but her inconsequential threat made him laugh more.

"Oh I do like a feisty woman!" he lusted, "Get back here you beauty!" Once again he forced her onto the sheets and climbed on top of her with ease. Holding her down with his strong forearm across her throat, he forced her legs apart as he struggled to undo his trousers.

Crying and screaming at the same time, seemed only to excite him even more as he pressed harder against her. She continued to wriggle and writhe beneath him and eventually freed one leg, which, with all her might, she brought up hard against his 'trinkets' and with a loud yelp and expletive he tried to catch his breath by which time, Louise had escaped his clutches. She ran to the door and frantically rattled the key to open it. Swinging it open to run along the corridor towards the stairwell, she stopped in her tracks as she caught sight of a young girl peeping out from behind a half opened door on the landing.

The figure darted back on realizing Louise had seen her. Hearing Partridge's steps across his bedroom, Louise shot into the same room, rapidly closing the door behind them as silently as possible, hoping he would not know where she had gone. Her legs were trembling as she thought her heart would explode. She could swear he would hear it pounding. Squinting through the half darkness, she looked at the young girl who stood immobile next to her, tears streaming soundlessly down her cheeks. Terror creased her face.

Turning towards her, she saw the fearful expression imprinted across her face, set deep into her eyes. Louise whispered as calmly as she could, "Shhhh. It will be alright. We shall be safe. Are you hurt?" The girl did not answer but continued to silently cry, as though she knew nothing else. "Has he hurt you?" she persisted. The girl nodded and rubbed her red eyes like a very young child. "Do not be afraid. Someone is coming for us." The girl made no reaction, as though numb. Trying to think what to do next, Louise tried to cajole her with reassurances. "Come, first, we must not make a noise. We are going to wait very quietly. Do you understand?" The girl just looked, vacantly.

Blaspheming, Partridge ran with clumsy footsteps along the corridor and past their door. The girl seemed frozen with shock or fear or perhaps she was devoid of understanding. Louise offered her hand and the girl hesitantly took it. Louise smiled encouragingly and beckoned her to follow close against her silk skirts, knowing they had little time to find an exit. Looking about the dark room, it was difficult to see to get her bearings. As her eyes became adjusted, she deciphered a bare room with bars at the window. There was nothing else except a basic iron bed and she could make out a pot on the floor. Not quite sure at first but with horror, she spotted manacles at the top and bottom end of the bed. Oh God! She felt sick.

She guessed he had gone back downstairs to look for her. With quickness of thought, she gestured to be silent and she risked opening the door. Half pulling the girl to stay close, she retraced her steps into his bedroom, remembering the key in the door. At least if she could get back in there, she could lock themselves in. Reaching the door, the girl pulled back fearfully and fought to retract her hand from Louise's, refusing to go in. Louise suddenly realized her terror. Dear God, this poor girl – what he must have done with her, heaven only knows. With no time to reassure her, she took her hand again and looked further along the corridor. Beckoning the girl to stay with her, she saw another open door.

Hurrying, she struggled with the reluctant girl until they were inside that room and forced the door closed. Acting quickly, she dragged any piece of furniture she could move until they were barricaded within.

There were no drapes at the window and so the frosty night

brought a clear sky and sufficient moonlight to enable her to see her surroundings. Fortunately, the room overlooked the drive at the front of the house. She prayed someone would come soon to rescue them and logically she needed to signal her whereabouts. Scanning the room, she saw a taper but there was no fire from which to light it. Louise gave an involuntary gasp of irritation, when she felt a slight tug at her sleeve. She looked round to see the girl pointing to the cupboard. Louise quizzically approached the hinged door and inside, found a small box of matches. "Oh, clever girl!!" she exclaimed almost silently. Striking a match, she managed to light the candle and placed it in the middle of the window sill, in the hope that should anyone come for her, they would see the flame.

Meanwhile at Bancroft House, Aunt Fee's carriage rolled up outside. Tobias gave a sigh of excited relief and had to admit to himself, he was relieved to have Louise back home. Lord Dorchester and Tobias went to greet everyone but could only see Aunt Fee entering the beautiful hallway fussing verbally about the weather and the carriage ride all in one sentence without drawing breath, whilst ungraciously allowing Elders to remove her shawl. Lord Dorchester greeted her and they made small talk as they stood awaiting Louise, surmising she was assisting Uncle Gerald from the carriage. Moments lapsed before she declared how her plan had come to fruition and she had made her diplomatic exit from Mr. Partridge's dinner party, to allow him and Louise to become better acquainted.

Grimacing, Tobias's stomach lurched and Lord Dorchester assessed the young man's reaction, unfavourably.

"You did what??" Furrowing his brows with incredulity, Tobias addressed Aunt Fee sharply. "Oh do not fear!" She laughed. "I have left her with uncle Gerald," she giggled again, "although he will not be in any fit state to trouble them!! Haha... I'm sure we shall have a wedding before long!!"

Tobias was enraged, mostly by fear. Lord Dorchester was deeply troubled by his reaction.

"Elders!!! Bring Isaac and Jake immediately – and get my driver to bring the horses too. He must then go directly into the village and bring the police. I believe Louise to be in grave danger. We must act immediately." Addressing Lord Dorchester, "Sir! Do you still keep a pistol for the animals?"

Aunt Fee looked astonished as she stood amidst a whirlwind of activity. She continued to babble reassurances, which fell completely on deaf ears.

"Is that truly necessary Tobias?" he floundered in the wake of Tobias's instructions. "Sir!...Please, where are the pistols? There is no time to explain my Lord but there are strange things afoot on your neighbour's land and we suspect him of cruelty or worse. I fear for Louise's safety."

Betsy heard the commotion upstairs and rushed into the hall, just as Aunt Fee had an attack of the vapours. Tobias rushed forward to prevent her heavy faint and Betsy instinctively grabbed the nearest chair and rammed it beneath the collapsing woman. From thereon in, she took charge of her care, acknowledging this with a nod to Tobias. Simultaneously she shouted for Rose to bring outdoor cloaks.

Jake came back into the hall reverently carrying two pistols. Tobias hurriedly reached for one and loaded it. Jake had never so much as held one before so happily deferred to farm boy Isaac to take the other. He seemed to know what he was doing with it.

Fetching some smelling salts to administer to Aunt Fee, Elders beckoned Violet and entrusted her with the task of caring for Izzy who had woken with the ongoing racket, probably wondering if it was Father Christmas arriving. He feared she might look through the window to see her uncle leaving the house armed with pistols. With horror written all over her face, Violet took two steps at a time to swiftly ascend the stairs.

Elders poured a glass of brandy for his master's shock. Lord Dorchester swigged it down in one then demanded a horse and against all recommendation, he too left the house.

A confused lull settled on the house along with a sense of troubled doom.

Chapter 24

Aunt Fee came to with a swirling head but nevertheless went straight into chatter about how she did not trust her host from the moment she encountered him!

Partridge ran about the downstairs of the house like a man possessed, shouting in his drunken stupour, calling for Louise, not by name but by any other filthy term, which came to his lips. At one point he stumbled and crashed into a highly polished table, causing the glassware upon it to slide off and shatter across the floor. Skidding on the shards of glass, he too ended up on the tiled floor on his backside, unaware of losing his wig in the fall. Pushing himself back up, he cut both hands badly but strangely seemed to feel no pain, despite the dripping blood and continued to search.

Uncle Gerald was oblivious to it all, yet the household staff heard all the commotion. They were very used to similar scenarios as his drunkenness and rages were commonplace but for that reason, were reluctant to go to his aid fearing their intervention would not be welcome. It was especially bad tonight and the staff feared for their own safety, not knowing in which direction his rampaging would turn. They stayed below stairs in the kitchen, keeping the door shut for as much safety as they could create, hoping tonight's escapade would soon be over. Hearing the woman's screams, there was one exception willing to investigate, however. Thunder.

Not finding Louise downstairs, Partridge decided to retrace

his steps upstairs, assuming she was playing some kind of hide and seek game. He crashed open each and every door, delighting in the chase and hopeful at each turn of a door handle, his prize would await him. His red face now dripping in sweat and his breathing was laboured. His footsteps were beginning to drag as he overexerted his energy.

The unknown girl clung to Louise behind the barricaded door as his footsteps drew ever closer. The girl's trembling worsened and Louise subconsciously held her breath as she tried to stay calm. The doorknob turned. He expected the door to swing open but instead, it jammed against the obstruction. He tried again with his shoulder to release the door. Still nothing moved. Fired up with anger now, realizing Louise's cleverness to hinder his attempts, he raged and with a final almighty shove of his full body weight against the door, the furniture behind it tumbled over as the door flew open, revealing both women facing him with their backs against the window and the flickering candle.

The majestic house stood against the wintry backdrop of a Christmas Eve sky. Under other circumstances, it could be perceived as beautiful. Tonight however, it seemed to hold terror. Tobias had a bad feeling. He, Jake and Isaac rode at speed up the hill towards the grand edifice, horses panting hard.

Drawing closer, they immediately saw the single candle, oddly blinking its flame in an upstairs window. They pulled up the horses to a halt outside and hastily dismounted, leaving the horses standing obediently to regain their breath, steaming in the cold night air.

Taking several hurried steps at a time, Tobias led the way up to the front door and without a second's thought, flung open the door and barged into the house, pistol in hand, with the other two on his heels.

Oddly, nobody was to be seen. The men stopped for a moment and listened. Snoring came from the front reception room. Uncle

Gerald was just as Louise had last seen him. Not that Tobias knew that, yet he cursed, realizing Louise was without protection, even from an old man.

Isaac drew Tobias's attention to the dripped splashes of blood leading to the stairs and upwards. Oh God!!!

Upstairs, finding both women together, Partridge was momentarily confused. In that next moment however, he relished the thought of taking them both in some sort of wonderful God given Christmas gift. Lurching towards them in his drunken state, he now realised the strength of two unruly wenches as they defended themselves with two pairs of clawing hands.

Trying to flee and push past him, he caught the girl easily with his strong arm and managed to pin Louise against the wall at the same time. He was not in the mind for letting either of them escape this game! He guffawed a filthy laugh. The girl froze to the spot, her heart hammering.

Frustrated now with their insubordinate behaviour, he roared ferociously. Rummaging inside his cummerbund he pulled out a knife. The girl screamed and pulled back, fearing for her life. Separated now, he yanked Louise towards him and knocked over a chair as he brandished the blade. He hauled Louise to one side in a strangle hold. Louise shouted to the girl to run but she could not move. She seemed to be looking over Louise's shoulder, beyond Partridge.

All three men heard a thud from upstairs and heeded Tobias's frantic instructions. Jake must stay in the hall to direct the police when they arrived and told Isaac to stay a distance behind him until he assessed the situation. They followed the sound immediately, heading upstairs.

Tobias heard a scream but felt sure it was not Louise. Confused, he hesitated for just a split second then regaining his direction, crept silently along the upstairs corridor towards the sound.

Reaching the open door, he was not prepared for the sight before him and he stopped in his tracks. To his utter horror, as he rounded the corner to enter the semi dark room, he saw Partridge standing by the window, with his arm locked around Louise's neck and a knife to her throat. A young girl was staring beyond them in sheer terror, as she looked towards the door at Thunder, pointing a gun at Partridge.

Fierce dialogue exchanged between the two men. Louise and the girl both saw Tobias behind Thunder, he too held a pistol. He gestured with a finger to his lips. The men were more absorbed in feisty exchange than to notice his presence.

Thunder could take it no longer. He was sick of being bullied and coerced into a life of crime and fear. He would rather come clean to the police and be thrown in jail than live his life as he had been. Somehow, Mr. Smythe had given him no choice but to tell the truth. He had suddenly felt guilty to realize what a bad person he had become and how weak he was for allowing Partridge to control him. He wanted Partridge to be gone. To rid him from his life, from everyone's life. It would only take one bullet, then he could bury him with the others. He was already a murderer so one more would make no difference! Partridge would just disappear just as he had seen Partridge do to others time and again. How good it felt to hold a gun towards him and threaten him with his life, just as he had done to others. Thunder felt good. Seeing Partridge without his wig, made him look old, weak, pathetic. For the first time in his life Thunder felt in control, strong. Yes, he could squeeze this trigger and end it all!

Lord Dorchester rode much slower than the younger men, despite his desperation to get there but arrived almost at the same time as the police who raced ahead of him into the house.

Partridge was intent on making Louise realize he was the master here. Nobody threatened him. He was the one who was in control. Thunder could never pull that trigger. He would disgrace himself before he could ever be a man. Nevertheless, he pinned her throat with the knife a little harder, threatening to slit it, unless he dropped the gun. "You'll never have the guts to kill me. You're nothing but a feeble weakling. You could not even kill a fly!!" He laughed grotesquely.

Isaac and the police were now in earshot and steadily moving forwards along the corridor towards the room. Tobias turned and signaled to wait. Thunder found his nerve to dare to contradict Partridge. Puffing out his chest importantly, "You forget" he reminded him, "I already killed that private detective in them woods!!"

Partridge burst out laughing. "You still think you killed him?!!"

Clearly finding this hilarious, "You absolute imbecile!!! YOU didn't kill him!! I DID!! It was great fun making you think you had! You should have seen your face!! All you had to do was bury him - and you didn't even do that for yourself!! You managed to get a sniveler to do that for you!! Did you think I didn't know?? Nothing gets past me! Make you feel good did it eh? Bullying a weakling to do your dirty work. Did it make you feel like me? Eh? Like a proper man? You fool! If you hadn't been so bloody careless, we wouldn't have had the bloody private detective snooping around in the first place!! He had to go! I couldn't even leave that to you! No... I had to do the job myself...Still, he's there with all the others who got in my way. Quite a little grave yard we have out there 'eh??"

Thunder was incensed. "YOU!!... YOU... killed 'im???" He could barely believe what he was hearing. "But you did make me do all them things so you wudn't tell the peelers I killed 'im!" Angry now, realizing his hands started to shake at the thought of pulling the trigger.

Lord Dorchester crept up the staircase behind the police.

Taunting him again, Partridge scoffed, "Well done indeed man! Of course!! It was easy to scare you – easy to make you piss yourself! The only thing you are good for is digging holes and bringing me women!! Hahaha," he laughed at the idea again. "You'll never pull that trigger! In fact, I'll bet it isn't even loaded! So why don't you just go to hell and leave me with these two beauties to have my fun!"

The standoff was unbearable. Thunder felt like he could explode with rage. In one swift movement, he threw the gun on the floor and hurled himself towards Partridge, grabbing him in anger around his neck. Partridge instinctively let go of Louise to protect himself, trying pathetically to release Thunder's grip, as he pressed tighter, then tighter still. He turned blue and finally slid down the wall and landed with a heavy thud on the floorboards. Louise snatched the girl by the forearm and ran towards Tobias. He quickly whisked them from the room and away down the corridor to safety. Louise ran directly into the arms of her father.

The police moved forward now behind Tobias, seeing Partridge fall to the floor, still. Thunder stood back, looking at him, relieved – even proud - to have killed him.

Turning now towards Tobias, Thunder saw the Police and panicked. He rushed for the gun on the floor but Tobias blocked his way. The gun scooted across the floor.

Partridge still felt the knife beneath him. Quietly grasping it, he suddenly threw himself forward with all his might towards Thunder's body and stabbed him in the lower back. As he fell, he continued to stab him with gruesome delight. Tobias and the police rushed to Thunder's aid. All too late.

In that moment, one gunshot rang out. The gun fell from his own hand. Silence. Blood streamed from Partridge's temple. Dead.

Chapter 25

Aunt Fee and uncle Gerald set out to continue their journey, at first light on Christmas morning. There had been no mention of the night before and it was a rather uncomfortable atmosphere. Nevertheless, Tobias was charming as always, after all, Louise was now safe and back home. Louise ensured that her departing guests had everything they needed for their onward voyage. Lord Dorchester was brief but polite and stood at the door to wave them off.

Christmas day was, despite everything that had happened the night before, a day of relief, homely contentment and gratitude for everyone's safety. The staff had been wonderful in looking after Louise when she had returned home from the hideous nightmare she had lived through the night before. What is more, they welcomed and catered for Sally-Anne and her elder sister Florence as though it caused no extra work.

The police had located the young girl's devoted sister through Mr. Smythe and their impassioned reunion was utterly heart warming. Sally-Anne's scars, both emotional and physical, would take time to heal but to be safe and secure in the arms of her sister was the finest Christmas gift anyone could have given either of them. They were invited to stay at Bancroft House over the festive season or until they were ready to return to their own home, once Louise was happy that Sally-Anne was fit to return after her deeply scaring ordeal.

Izzy had a wonderful time playing with the toys Father

Christmas had left and she especially loved the doll, which Louise gifted her. She at least, was thankfully wholly oblivious to the recent terror, which had brought together this unlikely group of guests and simply enjoyed the extra young female company and innocently regarded them as 'new friends'. Joyously however, Tobias had given her the news, that Bouncer's owner was no longer able to look after Bouncer, so if she wished it, he could officially be her dog. She was ecstatic beyond words and simply knew that Father Christmas had had a hand in this wonderful gift.

Louise and her father kept family tradition and invited everyone to sing carols around the Christmas tree. Tobias surprised them all with his rich baritone voice which enchanted Louise and she believed she could have listened to him sing all night! Thanks to Betsy, they all delighted in eating an amazing goose dinner with all the traditional trimmings, in a makeshift but equally festive dining room. Louise marveled at how on earth she had managed to provide all of this with all the catastrophes surrounding them those past few days.

Sally-Anne and Florence ate with gusto, if little manners but that did not offend Louise at all. In fact, she found it a joy to see them enjoy their meal so readily and was glad she could offer them this at least, knowing that their poverty would have otherwise allowed them only frugal pickings. They had both been offered a tub to bathe in and some spare clothes donated by the staff, which Louise promised to replace. They had slept wrapped around one another on Izzy's 'make do' mattress transported to an upstairs room and Florence thought it was the kindest thing that had ever happened to them.

In the light of day, Louise cringed to see Sally-Anne's tortured body. The broken skin was infected on her right ankle and she could barely tolerate sleeves around her wrists. There were bruises here and there, even some around her neck. Louise had Betsy tend them, which she did with sweet compassion. It was with greater sadness that Louise realised that the girl did not speak. Louise did not know if this was through physical incapability or psychological trauma but suspected she had become so inhibited that she had become an elective mute.

Her sister was wonderful with her and had an innate understanding of how to comfort her. They clung to each other as though they never wished to be parted again, Sally-Anne finding complete security in her sister's arms and Florence offering full protection against the world.

It transpired that they had no longer any living relatives and lived in a ramshackle cottage on the perimeter of the village fields, towards Willersey. Florence, acted as both a mother and father to her younger sister, even though she herself could be no more than fifteen years old. When Sally-Anne was abducted, she was broken. She had no will to eat but spent all her energy from morning until night, day on day, looking for her sister. By chance one day, she saw Thunder. Recognising him, she followed him. She could not be sure that he went to the workhouse but it was worth a try. She managed to get to the perimeter of the building but was chased away. Trying again the next day, she hid behind the pig bins and saw an opportunity to slip in amongst a family as they arrived. Finally she broke through the doors and encountered the kindly Mr. Smythe.

Mr. Smythe was indeed very shocked to hear of the latest turn of events and the true extent and seriousness of his colleague's secret murderous life. Reflecting now, he did not believe that Thunder was innately a bad man but rather a misguided one who had succumbed to a life of corruption under Partridge's authority, who had artfully used blackmail, to keep him answerable. Smythe was of the opinion, that Partridge's demise was no loss to the world. In fact the world was a safer place without him. He was sorry too that his private detective had perished by the hand of this evil man and left his family in deep sadness and dire straights.

It was evident during the course of Christmas Day, that Lord Dorchester was developing something of a soft spot for the young Miss Izzy as he referred to her and before the day was out, she had been allowed to sit upon his knee in front of the fire, whilst he read a story from Louise's favourite childhood book. It was debatable who enjoyed the experience more!

Over the next two weeks, Tobias awaited the arrival of his own private detective to tie up some loose ends and look into the private life of Partridge's greed and criminality. The police had needed Tobias's and Isaac's assistance in locating the vicinity of the dead body they had encountered. They took with them Bouncer, who proved invaluable in finding the other three bodies which lay in the woods alongside Partridge's mansion. Tobias engaged the services of his friend to support the case of Jake in his unfortunate part in burying the private detective's body.

Tobias's business advisor also arrived at his request and they had a number of fruitful discussions related to the running of Broadway's Broadside Workhouse. Smythe, welcomed the notion of a new business partner, one who could help him take forward a new approach to the running of a more modern regime. He was extremely interested in Tobias's innovative ideas and along with Lord Dorchester's offer of financial support they began to develop a sound business plan.

Louise did not mind at all that Tobias and Izzy were caused yet again to stay at Bancroft House even longer, whilst police enquiries continued. The police had heard all Partridge's confessions that night but further investigations and body exhumations were essential in order to close the case.

Rose decided that she ought to go to pay a visit to her father's house and asked permission from Lady Louise to take some hours off work to do so. He had not been seen for quite some weeks and it had disappointed Rose, though not surprise her, that he did not come to pay her a visit at Christmas. Louise did not like the idea of her going alone, so suggested that Isaac accompany her, for safety.

It was with relief that Louise saw them safely back at Bancroft House but was curious to hear Rose's story. It seems that as they arrived at the old cottage, there were children playing outside and it all looked quite different. Rose walked up the pathway to find a young mother breastfeeding a baby up on the step, looking curiously at Rose. Rose had asked for her father, only to hear that he had moved from the house weeks ago, leaving it 'in a proper filthy state!" ...Rose was not at all surprised with that comment but was deeply shocked at finding he had gone.

Rose surprised herself to find she was really worried about him, for all that he had been cruel to her since her mother died, he was still her father, and she realized she did care for his safety. The woman had no idea where he had gone. Rose felt suddenly empty. Lost. Forgotten. Why would he just disappear and not tell her? Isaac had no idea how to console her, as he had been lucky enough to have come from a happy if poor family situation and could only imagine how devastated he would feel if this had happened to him. Rose wondered if perhaps she should have gone home sooner? Louise did her best to comfort her but could not shake off her own annoyance at her father for forsaking his only daughter.

Tobias still had not yet broached the sensitive subject of Izzy's guardianship with Lord Dorchester and this had been playing on his mind. Eventually one evening into mid January, he found the opportunity to ask him directly, why he had not mentioned the proposal to Louise, having given him the impression that he would.

Lord Dorchester was not expecting the question to come so

directly, although he knew Tobias would approach it at some point. A little taken aback, he began, "I had indeed intended to do so Tobias, just as I said I would but Louise was not in the right frame of mind at that time and I knew that had I made the suggestion, or even asked the question, she would have cast it out without good thought. I suggested she came here to Bancroft House to refresh her mind and soul and find her bearings in life. I believed giving her responsibility would make her realize her value and maturity and whilst I knew in my heart that she would be an excellent mother to the child, I decided that she would have to come to that conclusion herself after due consideration. I knew that if anyone could present the story as it should be told, it would be you. It was God's intervention which created the time and circumstance for her to get to know Izzy – and you!" He paused with thought... "I do believe that if you were again to ask the question, her answer would be different."

"It is no longer so simple, Lord Dorchester." Tobias replied. He had come to realise over the past weeks, that his initial plan was no longer viable. "I cannot now see how I could possibly hand over my darling niece to be cared for by a guardian. I must think seriously how I might plan for Izzy's future in a different way, with her best interests at heart. In addition, I have had time to reconsider my own life and ambitions and come to a conclusion ...but I need your blessing."

Lord Dorchester looked up from his brandy glass, across the top of his pince-nez and smiled.

The business meetings became more frequent over the next few weeks and plans were moulded to suit all. Smythe wanted to rid himself of the mantle of 'merciless administrator' who only sought profit from the destitution of others. He wanted pauperism to be dealt with in a dignified manner and workhouses to be a restorative place offering safety and security.

He wanted to rid the current trend where administrators turned a fine profit for themselves and housed the most vulnerable in society in cruel and prison like circumstances. They must remember to adhere to The Poor Law Amendment Act of 1834, where the poor should be helped to support themselves, since no able-bodied person could get poor relief unless they took up residence in a workhouse. He recognized that the workhouse was of course a grim place, where unfortunates would be required to work hard for their food and accommodation but there were those who troubled him greatly. These were the orphaned and abandoned children as well as the physically and mentally sick, the disabled, the elderly and unmarried mothers. Those around the table spent lengthy hours of discussion about how they could improve Broadside workhouse.

Tobias and Lord Dorchester fought hard from the same position, to segregate the young from the workhouse and provide them with stable and secure protection in a home where they would receive an education, which would be superior to that currently available in the workhouse.

Smythe was impressed by the compassionate commitment they were offering and ultimately, following a vote, it was decided: Broadside, would have a children's home, to accommodate the young of those parents who were committed to the workhouse.

The success was shared and celebrated with excitement at Bancroft House that evening. Louise was so proud of the two men in her life, that they had potentially achieved such a worthwhile innovative proposal and she knew how much this would mean to Tobias. He said he had been driven by his sister's memory and the suffering of his innocent and vulnerable niece and hoped that the home would become a flagship for others to follow and that the past would never be allowed to be repeated.

Louise saw how commendable this was but it left her intrigued about her father's motivation, as he too was impassioned beyond anything she had seen in him before. She listened to his reasoning and purposeful arguments and wondered where this desperate need had come from to protect these young children. Perhaps it was simply his love of his daughters – as she knew how very much, she and her sister were adored by him, yet there seemed to be something more, as though he himself had suffered at the floor of the workhouse.

Biding her time, she broached the subject gingerly, "Papa, it must have been so awful to enter through those gates these past few weeks to see for yourself the running of Broadside?" Her father reflected on the scenes he had witnessed upon his inspection of the workhouse. Nodding with sadness he confessed, "Indeed, dear daughter. The conditions were both grim and despairing. I saw how much it punished the mind of Tobias, to realise how badly his niece had been treated and to imagine the lifelong scars upon all of those children. We shall never know how deep and eternal those scars shall be. A heavy burden, indeed. I thank God for our good fortune, Louise, never to have been subjected to that life, for it is no real life at all but drudgery, pain and heartache. I could not bear the thought of you or Elspeth being subjected to such abuse, which I witnessed there. I pity the misfortune of little Miss Izzy but praise her uncle for his commendable efforts to protect her now and his endeavours to prevent such circumstance prevailing. He is a good man, Louise. We have much in common." He fell silent momentarily as though considering continuing.

Seizing the lull of opportunity she asked, "Papa... why did you not discuss with me the guardianship of Izzy?" She continued before he had chance to reply. "I have struggled to understand and it is so unlike you not to prepare me or advise me for such a request."

Sitting together, he bent forward and took her hand, folding it between his, gently rubbing the delicate skin across her knuckles, "Louise, do you remember Grandmamma Ellen?" He saw her quizzical look. "You would have been very young when she passed away!" Not understanding where this was leading, Louise confirmed, "Yes, Papa. A little." She sighed lightly reflecting on the scattered memories her name evoked. "I remember her white hair tied up on top of her head." Louise smiled at the memory. "Her beautiful brown eyes – so pretty. I picture her in a crisp white blouse ... and..." As though the thought came from nowhere, she said, "One night at bedtime... she said to me 'I hope you will never be afraid of the dark, my darling'. I never understood why she said that!" A moment's reverence passed between father and daughter. "Why do you ask, Papa?"

"Just before you left home," he began gently, "I came across some documentation, of which I knew nothing about. I took it to Tobias for verification and between us, we discovered that it was paperwork, which my father had kept, perhaps intending me to find it one day! It seemed that my own mother..." He took a deep breath and struggled to say, "suffered as a child, at the hands of a workhouse Guardian."

Louise gripped his hand as though to give him greater strength to deal with his deepest emotions. "Her parents, my grandparents, had fallen on hard times. It seems that the coal mine had closed following a bad accident, losing many men. Those surviving, needed to find more work and there simply were not enough jobs to go around. Many were left unemployed including grandfather. They were left penniless. My grandfather must have had no other choice but to turn to the workhouse. My heart breaks for him."

Louise found herself weeping tears of compassion for her great grandfather and her own dear papa in his distress now. "The script was difficult to read and patchy but between us, Tobias and I deciphered the bones of what had happened to the woman whose life was recorded in the paperwork. It seems she was punished hard both at work in the mill but also had been taken aside at night time for the pleasure of the guardian of the workhouse." With these words, he stifled a sob and a single tear was released down his cheek. Louise pained inside her chest and wept too.

"We were able to piece together the basic story and I thank the Lord that fortunately, my father came to the mill one day. He was a self made cloth merchant at that time and made much of his money doing so. The paperwork indicates that he fell for the beautiful girl he encountered one day. Her task was to 'hotpress' the textile between hot metal plates to finish the product. His job was to inspect the final product quality. He saw the burns on her delicate skin, the sweat she poured and the filth she endured and it seems he fell in love with her. She had been separated from her parents and never found them. After many visits, he offered to take her to his own employment and paid the guardian well to release her, so saving her from a life of horror.

She was but very young. My father was much older. It was seemingly much later that he discovered the true horrors she had endured and so documented all of this for posterity, with a prayer that this regime must stop! It was very clear, that he loved her dearly, as she did him."

He tried to explain further to Louise, "It was difficult at first to confirm to whom he was referring, as my mother took on a different name. She was so young when she was taken into the workhouse that she could not even write her own name. It transpires, that her name metamorphosed from Elizabeth by birth to Betty, as was commonplace but in her childish language it became Bunty. That is how it remained."

She was a wonderful woman, Louise: As graceful as she was gracious. A fine mother to her four children and the bond between my parents was tangible. They had held this dark secret until they died, believing it to be shameful. Like myself, my brothers and sister had no idea. So, my dearest Louise, perhaps that is why she hoped you would never fear the dark, as I imagine, she did!"

They sat in silence holding on to each other's hands and simply reflecting, perhaps praying. "So, my darling, forgive me for not discussing with you Tobias's proposal but you will see now that I would have been very biased in advising you. This revelation was and still is raw and I could not have been impartial. In addition, you were not in the most receptive of moods for new and challenging ideas and I knew that the best place for you to find your soul and come to terms with your own grief for your mamma, was to suggest you came here, to Bancroft House. It is here where you always felt most at one with yourself. In any case, if anyone could make you see the right way forward, I was certain it would be Tobias. This decision must be entirely yours but you know that, as ever, I am here to support you whatever that decision might be. I am blessed to have you as my darling daughter!"

Lord Dorchester stood and invited his daughter into his arms. There they stood in silence for some moments embracing as Louise shed her tears of love and understanding. Breaking the sadness, Lord Dorchester stood back purposefully and smiled. "Come, let us take a walk!" Bouncer, heard the significant word and came charging through from the hallway, tail wagging.

Chapter 26

Three womens' bodies were raised from the ground as well as the corpse of the missing private detective. As a result of investigations, it transpired that each of the three girls in turn, had been segregated from their families in a similar way to Sally-Anne, by abduction and admitted into the workhouse. From there, they had been singled out and coerced into "helping" Mr. Partridge at his home... On hearing this disgusting revelation, Louise realized that had they not gone to the house that night, Sally-Anne might well have been the next in a grave.

Of course, interviews were carried out with the staff at Mr. Partridge's home and it transpired very quickly that everyone without exception, was afraid of him and felt bullied into fulfilling unpleasant tasks and dared not deny him for risk of losing their job or being beaten. Some had indeed been physically tormented and punished. All had been abused in some way. There were a few amongst them who admitted to hearing the screams of the girls who then went missing. The reports made for gruesome reading. In addition, most had also been threatened, by Abel Theodore Cooper, a common thief, who had become Mr. Partridge's lackey. Teased and bullied in childhood for his gawky demeanour, booming voice and especially his middle name, he had become commonly known to all as Thunder.

Weeks rolled into months as they awaited the crown court

case. Tobias spent much time attending to paperwork on other matters and arranging meetings. He and Louise's father would scrutinize documents and prepare for meetings with business advisors, of which Louise knew little.

Finally, one spring day, they were all called to attend court. It was unusual that a trial would last longer than two days. Word of mouth around the village had however whipped up much interest, which spread far beyond those parameters and the whole affair became something of a spectacle. Newspapers were printing extra copies as their circulation increased because of headline news related to the story. It was rumoured that tickets were being issued as far as London, to diplomats and fashionable ladies who hoped to be seen, as they had heard about Mr. Woolmer's eligibility, handsome looks and courage. The Gloucester courtroom on the day was crowded and effervescent with excitement and tension.

There was much preamble. The Crown presented the case, informing the jury about the circumstance of the events, which took place on Christmas Eve, which ended in the deaths of Mr. William Albert Partridge and Mr. Abel Theodore Cooper.

The jury was to assess whether Jake Fitzgerald, Tobias Henry Woolmer or Isaac Arthur Kipling, were criminally involved with the abovementioned in the abduction, rape, murder and/or disposal of bodies found buried on the land of Mr. Partridge. Or if they were in any way connected with the abduction of Rose, or attempted kidnap of Lady Louise.

First on the stand was Lord Thomas Dorchester, who gave a witness statement.

Next, Tobias Woolmer then Isaac, were required to answer questions about finding the body in the woods, then subsequently their witness accounts of the deaths of the two men on Christmas Eve. Tobias's solicitor provided some evidence, which interested the jury and substantiated their accounts.

The private detective, appointed by Tobias to investigate the disappearance of the first detective and the suspicious behaviour of Mr. Partridge, together with the abduction of Rose, took to the stand next. His macabre findings left the courtroom in animated discussion. It was some time before the judge could quell the hubbub and bring order back to the stand.

There was a break for refreshments by early afternoon but it seemed that nobody was remotely hungry. The courtroom erupted with chatter and speculation. The fashionable ladies jostled for position to get access to Mr. Woolmer's vicinity to try to have him notice them but he was neither within reach nor interested. With frustration, they resumed their seats for the afternoon hearing.

Jake was waiting in the wings, terrified. It was difficult for him to revisit the events, which lead to his involvement in burying the private detective. He felt sick to be required to remember the feel of this man's lifeless translucent blue flesh as he manoeuvred his now almost stiff body. He had never before even seen a corpse but to handle a rigid cold human, was simply too morbid to bear. He dreaded that there could be a terrible miscarriage of justice and he could be sent to prison. He had read about such cases and feared that the clever barrister could wittily trip him up with his cross-questioning or twist his words and he could end up accused of being guilty. He would rather die than go to prison! This was his worst nightmare. Taking the stand, shaking, he was required to describe every grim detail of his first confrontation with Thunder and the fight in the woods, then worse, his encounter with the same man in the kitchen of the big house where he was bullied into doing Thunder's dirty deed and finally, recounting the ghastly digging of the grave, in ground which was rock hard with ice. Worse still, he had to admit to keeping this a secret.

It seemed like an age that he was on the stand but soon it was over and the turn of Sally-Anne and her sister Florence.

They were allowed in such unusual circumstances to go to the stand together. Florence answered most of the questions and explained Sally-Anne's loss of voice through trauma. Sally-Anne was asked questions, which permitted only yes or no responses, communicated with a nod or shake of her head. She was also required to show the court her still scared skin. She appeared lifeless or even non-comprehending. Her sister however, sobbed.

The distance away from Broadway forced the witnesses attending the court case to stay overnight in Gloucester. It wasn't until the next day, that Louise was required to present to court her version of events the night Thunder tried to abduct her. Despite her usual self-assurance and composure, today she was trembling, not because she feared being accused of any wrongdoing but just that she found the whole procedure, daunting. Once standing in the dock however, she spoke eloquently and with decorum. Her confident words fell impressively upon the ears of the jury.

However, she feared for Jake who had been a good and loyal servant, first to her father, then to her. It was all too bizarre that he should be involved in this fiasco. In addition, she fully understood poor Rose's nervousness. Rose had had a worse experience, in that Thunder actually managed to kidnap her and drug her. Louise watched later as Rose stood to take her turn to be questioned and was as proud of her as if she were her own child. Seeing her there, standing in the dock, facing the crowd of onlookers, Louise realized how much she had grown from the frail, under confident, shy, abused little girl she first met only months ago.

As Rose faced the courtroom to answer questions, her attention was taken from time to time, by a male figure sitting amidst the crowd. For some reason she could not help but keep looking across to that person. He seemed quite smartly dressed with a cap pulled down slightly over his eyes and he seemed to shift behind the person in front of him whenever her gaze flicked across the room in his direction. There was something about him that made her feel compelled to look again but she needed to keep her focus as best as she could on the questions she was being asked and forcing her mind to recall through the fog of memory the night she was drunk and later drugged.

Finally, Mr. Smythe was there, to give his side of the story. His educated manner and upstanding character added weight to the conclusion that Mr. William Albert Partridge had brought fear and pain to many people and his control over others, tormented the likes of Sally-Anne and the other girls who had been lost. Even Thunder himself had been influenced by the bullying techniques of Mr. Partridge and following his example, succumbed to his evil ways.

The newspapers fed on the grisly details for days but the final outcome of the court hearing was that, thanks to Tobias's solicitor and sound character references from Lord Dorchester and Lady Louise, Jake was cleared of any criminality in his involvement with the disposal of the body of the private detective.

Of course, Jake was immensely grateful for his reprieve and Violet believed she herself had never been so relieved. She had always believed in his innocence and now he was a free man without any doubt hanging over his head, she hoped he would one day look at her as more than a friend. At least they were that: good friends.

Tobias and Isaac were congratulated for their part in discovering the body in the woods and in addition they were verbally applauded for their courage in rushing to the aid of Lady Louise on Christmas Eve in the fear that she may have been in danger and rescuing her. Indeed, her life was in peril, as was that of Sally-Anne.

Tobias was above all, commended for his insight and astute

assessment Mr. Partridge's misconduct and subsequently his hiring of a private detective to intercept the gross negligence of the governor of Broadside Workhouse, who had disabused his role in society and neglected his duties which were laid out as orders and issued by the Poor Law Commissioners. Mr. Partridge was ultimately therefore found posthumously guilty of multiple murders, cruelty towards his employees in his care, corruption, exploitation, gross misconduct and abusing his privileged position in society.

A huge relief spread across the courtroom.

Chapter 27

Now that the court case was over, it was time to move on. Of course, at first, there had been much jubilation in celebrating a successful outcome of the trial. Justice had been done and courage had been recognized. However, a sadness slowly crept upon Louise as she anticipated both Tobias and Izzy leaving, to return to their home. How quiet the house would become! Her father too would no doubt be returning to their town house and she would be left with one of two options: Either to return with him and perhaps venture into London to visit Elspeth and the twins for a short while, or stay and continue the running of Bancroft House. Either way, her life was about to change.

Tobias was still conferring with Mr. Smythe regarding the setting up of a children's home alongside Broadside workhouse and her father too was involved in the planning. For the first few days after the trial, this took them away from Bancroft House for many hours of the day and Louise was able to spend some treasured time with Izzy. Louise loved these shared times and realized how precious they were becoming, in the knowledge that they were limited before she and Tobias left. They had developed a warm and natural bond, which Louise had begun to cherish.

Following the trial, Florence and Sally-Anne had tried to readjust to their former life but it quickly transpired that Sally-Anne found it very hard to sleep in what had been their familiar home. Upon returning there, Sally-Anne's cruel memories were too powerful to allow her to relax, feel comfortable, or above all, sleep. She was becoming exhausted and distressed and the lack of any sense of safety or security, took its toll and she again became mute. Louise was paying regular visits and on her latest visitation, became very concerned for Sally-Anne's mental stability. She looked increasingly more fragile and could no longer find the ability to work. Florence dared not leave her side, so she too was unable to work. Louise feared that in the first instance, without either girl being able to work, they would become so impoverished they too would by necessity, end up in a workhouse. In fact, Florence had confessed that she had resorted to stealing stale bread to stave off the hunger. Secondly, Sally-Anne's behaviour was worryingly deteriorating and she had begun to perform strange and unnatural routines. Louise worried that Sally-Anne might well instead, end up in a mental asylum.

The work on the new laundry room was almost complete and Louise had been considering taking on more staff. Perhaps this would be the opportunity to offer employment to the girls, which she could contrive to combine with accommodation. That way, she could keep her eye on Sally-Anne's health and being away from their dilapidated home with all its horrific memories, may give the young girl space and security to recuperate. Furthermore, Betsy's good food would give her the strength she needed. This would be her plan.

However, in the cold light of day, that plan now seemed rather a ridiculous idea with the honest realization, that very soon her household would be depleted with so many people leaving. The thought of it made her heart sink.

There was much to think about! Upon returning home that evening, Tobias suggested a walk around the gardens which Louise had been therapeutically reorganising, distracting her mind during the weeks of awaiting the court judgement. She had been developing a wonderful walled garden for the kitchen to be able to access their own fruit and vegetables, which was now beginning to flourish but passing through this, via an arched walkway, they could already smell the sweet frangrances of roses in a further garden. Set out in geometric style, it had become a peaceful haven to sit, reflect and re-energise.

In synch with each other and without tangible communication, they both took a seat upon a stone settle to absorb the pleasure of the garden and allow their senses to be calmed by the gentle scene: Bees about their business in and out of the rose petals, a flitting butterfly floating on a mild movement of early summer's air and the nearby mellow, fluted sound of a blackbird.

Glancing sideways towards her, Tobias encouraged, "You have something on your mind, Louise. What is it?"

"Goodness, you know me well!" she replied.

"We have spent considerable time together these past few months, have we not?"

"Indeed! But I suspect that you will tell me you must soon leave. I believe you have achieved all you needed to do here and I am so pleased that you have fulfilled your ambitions regarding Broadside workhouse. Your sister would be proud of you!"

"Thank you, Louise, but I have not achieved quite all that I first set out to achieve though, have I?" he looked directly into her eyes. She knew exactly to what he was referring.

"No. You have not... but neither do I believe that your request would have been concluded in the right way for Izzy's best interest, Tobias, had I agreed."

"How do you mean Louise? Are you saying that you would not make a wonderful guardian for my niece?"

"I am saying that whilst she is the most wonderful child and I have grown to adore her, she needs her devoted uncle in her life and around her permanently. This is in HER best interest! It is

YOU who have made her the beautiful little girl she has grown into. It is YOU who must take the credit for this and it would break her heart for you to leave her with anyone else, no matter how much they would grow to love her and look after her. I do also believe, that it would break YOUR heart to leave her!"

Tobias nodded solemnly and bent forward to reach for her hand. She had become used to that sense of her stomach plummeting when he touched her and the tingle his hand left beneath her skin. She flushed red and returned his gaze. "You are right Louise. Of course! So you will not be angry with me if I now retract the request? You will not think me a worse person for believing you should not be Izzy's Guardian? That she should stay with me?"

Louise felt her eyes prickle with pending tears and averted her gaze. "I am glad that you will stay by her side, Tobias. She could not ask for a better, more loving and caring guardian." She feigned a weak smile even though her heart felt like it was shattering into a thousand pieces. Wanting to run back to the house, throw herself on her bed and weep for England, she clenched her jaw tight and stood to make her exit, turning to go as elegantly as possible.

In that same moment, Tobias also stood and grasped at her hand to halt her steps. "Louise. Stop. Hear me out."

There was a moment's confusion in Louise's mind. She simply stared back at him.

"My Darling..." He slowly shook his head. Louise sucked in her breath in surprise to hear such a term of endearment pass his lips. "I am not asking you to be Izzy's guardian," taking a deeper breath and raking back his hair in that familiar way that always took away Louise's breath, he continued, "because I have grown to love you so very much over these past few months – in fact from the first day I met you, I have been besotted!" He smiled at the thought of his schoolboy confession! "I cannot see how I can have a future without you in it. You are right – Izzy needs me – but I need you!! ... and I know you will make such a good mother to her! She already loves you and I believe you love her too."

Holding both her hands in his, he bent to one knee. Spellbound by the sincerity in his eyes and earnest plea in his voice, she heard his unexpected words, "Please Louise, I would be honoured if you would agree to being my wife and a mother to Izzy. We can be an instant family.... and I hope, maybe, have children of our own?" He continued to look directly into her beautiful eyes, as she stood expressionless, immobile, holding her breath, her mind catching up on the words he had just spoken. A single tear overspilled to trickle down her cheek.

In that heartstopping moment, he fearing she would turn him down, as she had done before. He dipped his head and closed his eyes against the thought, then standing to hold her closer, he begged in little more than a whisper, "Louise, I cannot bear for you to say no!... PLEASE," he implored, "say you will marry me!"

Louise thought she might actually combust with happiness. Lord Dorchester had already willingly given his blessing to Tobias and there was no doubt at all in his mind, that he was the perfect match for his darling daughter. The household rejoiced in the news and there was a euphoric sense of celebration enfolding them all.

Both Louise and Tobias immediately sought the approval of Izzy. She was found near the barn amongst the chickens, chatting to them like old friends, with Bouncer at her heels. As they approached, hand in hand, Izzy looked up, squinting into the sunshine, instinctively sensing something different about them.

"Izzy, come and sit a while! Louise and I would like to talk to you."

Dutifully, the child followed them to a rustic bench propped up against the barn wall, giving shade to Purrcillus curled up beneath. Tobias lifted her onto his knee. "Darling," he began, "do you remember when we first came here and I explained that it was not always possible for me to look after you on my own and that we were hopeful that Lady Louise might act as a guardian to you? Do you recall us talking about this? ..." Izzy tilted her head to one side and nodded, thoughtfully. Tobias continued, "Well, we have had a wonderful time staying here and getting to know Louise haven't we and..."

Izzy interrupted unexpectedly. "Has Father Christmas been?" she asked excitedly.

The question stopped Tobias in his tracks. It was so bizarre, that it completely took Louise by surprise. Louise interjected, trying to rationalise Izzy's thoughts. "Izzy, Father Christmas only comes in December... you remember that don't you? We are in the summer now."

Suddenly, a memory flicked through Tobias's mind. Remembering the slate, Tobias realised from where the question had come.

"Ahh!" He said, smiling. "I understand!" Surreptitiously squeezing Louise's hand and offering her a clandestine wink of his eye to suggest she bore with him, he continued to address Izzy. "It would indeed seem that Father Christmas might work in magical ways, would it not Izzy? Do you think that you would like to share your most precious secret with Louise?"

Louise was by now quite perplexed but listened intently to what Izzy had to say.

After some fidgeting, Izzy started, "Lady Louise, I sent a message to Father Christmas... I drew a picture on the slate you gave me..." Izzy became shy and dropped her head, squirming a little on Tobias's knee with embarrassment. Prompted by Tobias, she continued. "I drew a picture of you and Uncle Tobias getting married..."

Louise, smiling, shot Tobias a surprised look. Tobias urged Izzy on, "And...what else Izzy?" "...and I asked Father Christmas to help make it happen." She shyly blushed to admit.

"Oh I see!" Louise threw her head back and laughed.

Taking them both by surprise now, "And, I wished it when I stirred the Christmas pudding too but I had to keep that a secret or it would not come true!", she grinned.

Tobias continued, although he felt that for all that he had planned to say to Izzy, she had pre-empted it all. "Well, I am not sure how much Father Christmas, or the christmas pudding, has had to do with this but I am so happy to tell you Izzy, that Louise has agreed to marry me!"

Of all the questions Izzy may have asked next, her first one took them both by surprise again. "Does that mean I can call her mamma?" Izzy asked shyly.

Louise could have melted with joy. Hugging the little girl close to her and kissing the crown of her head, "Of course, if that is what you would like, dearest child, but we shall never forget your real mamma, for she will always be in your heart." Izzy thought this to be perfect.

Chapter 28

Life was good! The sisters were eternally grateful to Louise for giving them this opportunity and already Sally-Anne was making tiny steps forward, improving in both mental and physical health, her appetite much improved. Rose felt very grown up and important in her new role as supervisor of the two new members of staff. She was much more self assured these days, following the trial and was as attentive and sensible as Louise could have hoped for. Her 'promotion' had instilled in her a certain maturity, which suited her and Louise knew that employing the two sisters had also brought a certain positivity to the other staff. Isaac, in particular, seemed to take a shine to Sally-Anne and it was plain to see that this was reciprocated.

Rose was in the new laundry area, showing both Sally-Anne and Florence the ropes, when across at the side of the house, there was a resounding knock at the kitchen door. Betsy opened it. She faltered as she tried to recognize the person standing in front of her.

"Hello Betsy. I trust you remember me? It has been some time since I visited! Do you think I might speak with Rose?"

"C-Come in" she stammered, disbelieving her own eyes. "Take a seat." She found herself staring rudely at the person in front of her. Distracting herself, she called for Jake, who came into the kitchen from the storeroom and said good morning to the visitor without recognising him. Betsy told him to go fetch Rose immediately.

Jake found Rose demonstrating how to use the new mangle so as not to catch fingers between the rollers. She was so engrossed in her task that she jumped to hear Jake speak. "A visitor?" she questioned. "For me?" Jake shrugged and nodded at the same time.

Walking into the kitchen, Rose hesitated, doubtingly, as she faced her visitor. Recognizing the man before her but in disbelief at what she saw. Suddenly, her mind flashed back to the courtroom and the person she was so drawn to, in the crowd. His hair cut, cleanly shaven, standing tall. He had now removed his cap as a gentleman should, twirling it between his hands slightly nervously. Cleanly pressed clothing. Leather shoes, highly polished.

"Father?" she questioned incredulously

"'Tis I!" he confirmed.

"I barely recognise you! You look ... you look so different! You look so well!"

The man smiled. "I have a great deal to talk about, Rose. Will you make time to listen? I know I do not deserve your attention but I wish to make amends for all that I have failed in." He turned to Betsy, who was trying her best to mind her own business and not at all succeeding, "Miss Tyler, please may you excuse Rose for a short while, so that we may talk?" He now spoke with such improved eloquence, even if stilted in his efforts.

Knowing that Lady Louise would not wish this man to take Rose out of her sight, whether or not he came dressed like a gentleman, she considered her answer carefully.

"How about I make you both a nice cool drink and you take a seat outside on the bench?" Betsy would be able to see them both from where she stood in the kitchen and was determined not to let them out of her line of vision.

"That is very thoughtful of you Miss Tyler. I am very grateful." With that, he politely opened the door for Rose to precede him.

Betsy saw them take a seat hesitantly next to each other in the sunshine. She sent Violet out with a tray of fruit drink and biscuits. She heard them laugh.

Some time later, father and daughter stood to face each other. He touched his daughter's shoulder briefly without her cowering, before passing her a small package. He spoke a few more words. Replacing his cap, he smiled, nodded goodbye, then walked away without a backwards glance. Rose watched him go. As did Betsy.

Tobias and Lord Dorchester arrived home in jubilant mood, after a full day of meetings. Tobias called for Violet to ask Lady Louise to come in from the garden as they had some exceptional news.

Louise came rushing in, taking off her gardening apron, making a pretense at tidying her hair and inspecting her broken nail all in one movement. "Whatever is it?" she asked excitedly. Tobias rushed to greet her, picking her up and swinging her wildly around the room. "Stop!!" she giggled, not really minding at all, "You shall make us both dizzy!!!" ...

Almost in one sentence, without stopping for breath, Tobias babbled through their news, whilst Lord Dorchester stood by enjoying the moment and smiling benignly. Tobias breathlessly revealed, that he had been appointed as co-guardian of Broadside workhouse, alongside Mr. Smythe. Louise jumped up and down with sheer joy but as though that were not enough, Tobias continued. In addition, his proposal to provide a home for the children of the same workhouse, had been accepted by the board and the detailed plans to proceed immediately, were also approved. In order to make this happen, Lord Dorchester had generously put forward a great deal of money to fund the purchase of Mr. Partridge's house, with the intention of turning it into such a home. Louise could have burst with excitement and laughingly rushed to hug both Tobias and her father in one fell swoop. Tobias continued his jabbering, adding as a matter of detail, that the house would no longer be known as 'The House on the Hill' but 'Mount Pleasant'.

At that point, Louise's father chipped into Tobias's animated monologue, to explain to Louise that in order to release such funding, he had decided to sell the family town house and retire here to Broadway. Louise was so proud of her father for making this choice. It must have been a difficult decision for him but she fully approved of his judgment and determination. She hugged him again with loving approval. Such wonderful news all around!

Louise now understood how tirelessly the men had been working behind closed doors for months, in order to reach this achievement. She admired the passion, which prevailed between them both and their mutual deep need, to change so many wrongs. Now, with a sense of relief and hope, they had a chance for justice to prevail and the ability, with much hard work ahead, to offer protection, security and a better life for those who would come through the doors of Mount Pleasant. Louise could not be more proud of them.

Rose carried the tray of used vessels back into the kitchen to wash them and to thank Betsy for her kindness. She couldn't wait to open her parcel, which she had safely secreted into her apron pocket and at every opportunity amidst her chores, she would check to see if it was still securely there.

Betsy's curiosity could take it no longer. "Well, are you going to open it then?" Rose was taken aback. "Open what?"

"Oh for goodness sake! Open the parcel your father gave you!... Go on then, open it!!" Betsy encouraged.

With gentle care, Rose withdrew the small package from her apron pocket. Placing it on the wooden surface of the kitchen table, she stared at the carefully wrapped brown paper parcel, tied with string. She stood back for a moment almost as though she did not know how to undo it, or perhaps did not want to.

"Well, go on then!" prompted Betsy with impatience.

Revelling in the joy of a rare gift, she reverently began to untie the string. Another pause, while she wiped her tremulous hands on her apron, before tenderly unwrapping the parchment. It revealed a small box. Totally absorbed now in her task, she diligently lifted its lid. With a gasp, her hand flew to her cheek and she briefly glanced upwards to Betsy. Returning her sight to the box, she slowly withdrew the most beautiful silver chain she had ever seen. A small piece of paper fell out. The appallingly written message read "So yer can wore yer mams gift." Unable to stop themselves, both women broke into tears. "Oh Betsy!!"... Betsy strode two steps forward and held this young woman until her sobbing stopped.

Both men and Louise were studying huge sheets of plans across the table in the salon, enthusiastically discussing the renovation ideas for Mount Pleasant, when a knock came to the door. Sally-Anne, for the first time, had brought a tray of refreshments sent up by Betsy. Louise was delighted to see her confidence had grown sufficiently to attempt such a task and welcomed her into the room with delight. A greater surprise followed. Sally-Anne spoke! Just a few words but...she spoke! Louise was overjoyed to hear her little voice again and the girl beamed with pride for herself. She simply passed on a message: "Lady Louise," she struggled, "Rose would like to speak with you." It was staccato and had clearly been rehearsed but nonetheless, a commendable effort and wonderful progress. "Of course, Sally-Anne." Louise smiled, playing her part in this first dialogue. "Please tell her, I shall come to the kitchen shortly." Sally-Anne bobbed a curtsy, feeling proud of herself and turned to leave the room. Before she reached the door, Louise called after her, "Sally-Anne. Well done!"

By the time Louise reached the kitchen, the tears had ceased but emotion still hung in the air. Louise could see immediately that Rose had been crying.

"Rose?" Louise was startled to see Rose apparently distressed. "You are upset! What has happened?"

Betsy, dipped a curtsy and diplomatically left the kitchen, muttering about tidying the pantry.

Walking towards the table, Louise noticed the brown paper packaging. Rose was clutching a small box. "Rose?"

"No Lady Louise, I am not really upset, just..." Rose could not find the words to explain her emotions. "My father came to visit today. I did barely recognize him! He looked ... sort of 'posh'. Was dressed clean and came to say he was sorry for all he had been to me and wanted to know how proud he was of me having this job. That's why he has not been to visit me. He has been trying to make himself better. Stopped drinking. Wanted me to be proud of him like he is of me."

Shocked at what she was hearing, Louise listened intently without interrupting, whilst Rose took a deep breath to continue. "He used the first few lots of my wages you gave him, to get smart so he could get a job. He did not collect the rest as he felt he did not deserve it. He is working now, m'Lady!" Rose added proudly. "He admitted he had followed me a few times, just to watch me ... see I was ok... I sensed it but thought I had been imagining things. ... I thought I saw him in the courtroom but could not be sure ... he looked so different. I did not believe it could be him!" She shook her head slowly as though she still could not credit the idea. "He told me he had never been so proud of me when he saw me take the stand and he wanted to stand up and shout to everyone that I was his daughter. Then he said ... he could have wept to hear how I was abducted and he was not there to protect me. I knew he could barely speak them words he felt so bad." Rose was again close to tears as she spoke.

Louise waited patiently, while she finished her story. "Lady Louise, he is trying so hard. He seems truly sorry for treating me like he did. He said he missed my mother so much and just didn't know how to cope when she died."

Passing the small precious box to Louise, "He gave me this m'Lady." Louise accepted the box as if it was an injured fledgling and opened its lid with gentle care. She saw the scribbled note. "What does this mean, Rose?" she asked curiously.

"M'Lady, my mother gave me her precious necklace as she drew her last breath. I cannot wear it because the chain is broke, so..." she bowed her head and the tears flowed. "He said he was giving this so that I could wear it always. Said it was the least he could do, to say sorry."

"Rose. Rose... has your father asked to see you again? Does he want you to go back to live with him?"

"No m'Lady, he said it would be wrong of him to ask. He knows I am happy here and looked after proper, like I deserve, he said. But he wanted me to know he was trying to be a better man. He wanted to make it right. Said he hoped he could see me now and then, if I'd let him."

"Rose, this is indeed extraordinary news. You should be proud of yourself that you have inspired your father to make himself a better man. He has clearly made a good start. I am so pleased for you to have seen him looking so well and..."

Isaac came crashing into the kitchen shouting for help. Please someone come! Quick!!!! It's Sally–Anne...I don't know what's the matter with her. She's screaming with pain, she's on the floor..."

Betsy heard the commotion and she quickly followed Lady Louise and Rose, as Isaac led the way to the barn. It seemed that Sally-Anne had gone out to feed the chickens and collapsed suddenly amongst a pile of straw. When they got there, she was clearly in much pain. Betsy rushed to her side and tried to calm her. Louise instructed Rose to go fetch Florence and Isaac to wait outside of the barn in case they needed him to fetch anything else.

Louise knelt down alongside Sally-Anne to comfort her as best as she could and try to assess what was the problem. She spoke with gently soothing words. The poor girl was shaking from head to toe with shock. The pain came again and she gave a scream that came from her very soul. Louise held her tight as the girl clawed at her mistress's arm with utter distress.

They heard feet running across the yard and in the next moment, Florence swung around the barn door and rush to her sister's side. Instinctively, she held her hand and brushed back her hair from her brow.

Between the three women, they managed to get Sally-Anne into a more comfortable place, propped up against the barn wall and realized she was bleeding heavily. It was now clear from Sally-Anne's slumped position on the floor, that her stomach was swollen and Betsy quickly assessed the situation and glanced knowingly at Louise. The girl was terrified and sobbing between each bout of pain. It was not clear whether Sally-Anne understood what was happening. Louise hurriedly dispatched Isaac to ride into the village to bring the doctor, urgently. As an after thought, she called out, "Please send Violet!"

Louise turned to Florence and asked, "Did you know?" Florence seemed just as shocked, "No m'Lady, I did not." She reflected for a moment then added, "She had been quite sick some weeks ago but I thought it was after all she had gone through and the horror of returning to our home where it all began! Oh please God... let her be alright. Will she be alright?" She looked to Louise for reassurance. Sally-Anne was oblivious to the conversation around her and just begged for them to make the pain stop.

"She's so very young Florence." Louise whispered, "I have sent Isaac to fetch the doctor urgently. Keep comforting her. That is what she needs and all we can do at the moment." She turned to Sally-Anne, "I have sent for help, Sally-Anne. The doctor will be here as soon as possible. You must try to keep calm. We are all here to help you." Rose came back in the barn. Thoughtfully, she had brought the blanket from her own bed. "I thought she looked cold, m'Lady. Did I do right?"

"That is very thoughtful Rose. Well done."

Violet arrived, concern written across her face. She had delivered two of her nieces, so had some experience in natural birthing but had never seen anything as awful as this before. She was very good however, at making Sally-Anne more comfortable and reassuring her with soothing words and helping her to breathe better through the pains.

They all sat there with Sally-Anne for longer than an hour. The pains grew worse and more frequent. Concern grew for Sally-Anne's safety. She writhed about on the floor and sweat dripped from her forehead. She still bled. Her wet hair plastered to her scalp. Her cheeks fiery red. She had been sick. After what seemed an eternity, the doctor arrived, with Isaac leading the way but the women quickly told him to leave as it was no place for a young man.

Throwing his bag to the floor in haste, the doctor took brief details of her history, given by Louise and Florence filled in the story so far, since her collapse in the barn.

After a brief examination, the doctor was confident of the diagnosis. He had seen this before but not in one so young. He had concluded that the baby was growing outside of the womb and the young girl was in grave danger. It may already be too late to save her. They needed to prepare an area for him to operate. It gave a small chance of her surviving but if they did not do this urgently, she would lose her life for certain. A quiet panic enveloped them all.

They would need to somehow get Sally-Anne to the kitchen and put her upon the kitchen table, prepared with clean white sheets. Louise dispatched Isaac to get Jake to assist in lifting her gently there, carrying her on a strong sheet between them and required Violet to advise both her father and Tobias of the unfolding drama. Rose was sent ahead to make sure everything was correctly prepared according to instruction, by providing copious amounts of hot water, spare sheets and extra cloths.

Each of them was allotted a specific task to assist in the emergency operation and they keenly but nervously took on their assigned roles. Florence was by instinct, already by her side to calm her, even though she herself, was in a state of profound shock. The doctor required Betsy to competently assist in the administration of both alcohol and opium and once Sally-Anne was deemed to be in a sufficiently soporific state to proceed, he made his first incision. Rose passed out.

Assuredly, the doctor completed the difficult operation, leaving Florence jittering and weeping but praying her little sister's life was saved. The next hours into days would be critical. Leaving instructions for her care, the doctor left but would call daily.

It was too difficult to transport Sally-Anne to the upstairs bedroom, so, hurriedly, a day bed was prepared in the parlour, where Jake had made a comforting fire, despite the warmth of the summer's day. Isaac could not do enough to help. He clearly had developed feelings for this young girl and cared very much for her.

Hours later, after all was done, Louise broke down sobbing behind closed doors in the arms of her beloved Tobias. Her heart broke for this child who had been horrifically abused throughout her short life and known fear, pain and sadness for most of her days. She knew she had done as much as she could for these two young women but feared it had not been enough. Sally-Anne was so fragile, her life hung in the balance. Her sister praying for her survival, as did Louise herself.

Over the next two days, the entire household acted out a

grand charade of normality. Everybody, except for Florence who never left her sister's bedside day or night, went about their daily business. Betsy routinely cooked good food but people barely ate. Violet performed well as a nurse impeccably following both the doctor's and Betsy's instructions. Rose kept up an impressive job of household chores beyond her own, whilst Jake and Isaac continued in their respective roles without prompting. The house ran like clockwork. Tobias spent his time occupying Izzy to keep her from realizing the sense of impending doom within the walls and Lord Dorchester set to on urgent paperwork for Mount Pleasant. Louise found enough resolve to appear outwardly composed and perhaps even unperturbed but inside she felt deeply forlorn and helpless, unable to sleep and without appetite. And so it was, that during those days, a heavy cloud descended upon the entire house.

Florence shed so many tears that she could cry no more. She sat by her sister's bedside and held her hand, combed back her hair with her finger tips and spoke gently of happier days. Such outpouring of emotion was in itself a cathartic release for Florence, purging her own soul of guilt and depression, sadness and failed hope. Her own sense of helplessness was overbearing and knowing how close to death her sister could be, she could not imagine life without her. The thought was simply intolerable.

By the third day, there was finally hope that Sally-Anne was through the worst. She was beginning to respond to Florence's dialogue and there had been lucid moments and eye contact and even a moment's smile. Everybody's spirit felt lifted and they all began to breathe again, feeling that life was returning to normal.

The weather had turned gloriously hot and Louise felt justified by the good news to spend some time in the garden, tending her flowering plants. She found this a wonderful form of escapism and could clear her head of worry, just for a short time. Tobias brought Izzy to see her and they spent some time enjoying the pleasures of the fresh air. They wandered along the pathways of vibrant coloured blooms and Izzy was keen to learn about the flowers around her. Some deeply fragrant pink carnations were overhanging the pathway and Izzy asked to pick them for her friend Sally-Anne, to help her recover. Louise smiled at the kind thoughtfulness of this beautiful child and she of course approved of the idea. In that moment, she thought of the meaning of carnations: 'motherly love' and smiled to appreciate yet again, that this sentiment was exactly what she felt for this child in front of her.

Later that day, however, when Sally-Anne's wound was tended to, as it regularly was, it was becoming noticeably hot to the touch and appearing swollen and red. In the event that this might occur, the doctor had left an iodine preparation, which was almost unbearably painful when applied and Florence could not stand to hear her sister's screams.

By the next day, Sally-Anne had developed a fever and needed constant care. Her tiny frame appeared further emaciated after days of lack of food and she grew so pallid, her skin looked almost translucent. She was barely able to take forced sips of water with drops of a soothing elixir Betsy had lovingly prepared, approved by the doctor. As Sally-Anne grew worse, the doctor came as soon as he was summoned and he prepared them for the worst. Disbelieving she could be deteriorating after seeming to improve, Florence refused to accept his words of caution. With all her inner strength, she willed her darling sister to get better. Propping her up, supporting her with her own arm, she tried to coax her with drops of water, mopping her forehead with tenderness, praying with every conscious thought, believing she was looking better.

Eventually recognizing Sally-Anne's body was resembling little more than a rag doll, Florence held her close in her arms with natural tenderness and reluctantly accepted, that her sister's breathing had become shallow and ragged. Finally, her body was spent and she had nothing left to fight with. Florence sobbed as she prayed for the soul of this sweet, gently child as she drew her last breath with a final gasp and slipped away into oblivion.

Devastated, Bancroft House sadly mourned her loss.

Chapter 29

It was a gloriously cold, crisp winter's day. Clear blue sky and glistening sunshine across a frosty backdrop. Evergreens and berries were wrapped in abundance, decorating the arched doorway of St. Eadburgha's church from where Louise and Tobias emerged euphorically, as the campanologists gleefully struck out the bells above them. Dried petals were strewn into the air and fluttered down onto their shoulders, as their guests whooped with joy. Laughter and smiles were infectious. A day of rejoicing. Louise's father had picked up Izzy so she could better see above the small group of well-wishers, as they waved off the newly weds in their fine carriage, setting off for their special first night of married life. Izzy, wearing the most fairy tale gown she ever thought possible to wear, had been promised a special, celebratory tea party at Bancroft House, with the staff and Bouncer and Purrcillus as her exclusive guests.

It was true: The incumbents of Bancroft House had recently surfaced from some very dark days indeed but those were all in the past now and after a period of respectful mourning for Sally-Anne, Louise and Tobias looked now to a brighter future where kindness and loyalty would prevail. They promised to support each other, in striving to right wrongs in society and especially to care for the most vulnerable, offering them security, trust and a future. They never doubted that they would succeed in this commitment to each other, to achieve those dreams and ambitions, because what they both most believed in, was love.

About the Author

Gail Fulton has recently moved to the Cotswolds with her husband and Border Collie, Monty. Their two daughters and a future son-in-law have also relocated to the area and they look forward to many hours of dog walks, dining out and laughter.

Gail has now retired from teaching but has also always been passionate about interior design and loved setting up their new home. Floral art is also one of her favourite hobbies too but another, is people watching! Gail gained an M.A. in Psychology, focusing her interest on personality development and she is still intrigued in body language, so loves her visits to coffee shops and observing behaviour. She and her husband delight in gardening and have created a wonderfully colourful space for socialising and relaxation. Together they love to explore the Cotswold countryside and have, over the decades, travelled extensively around the world, finding inspiration for her writing. Gail has since childhood, loved to write. Her repertoire has largely covered childrens' stories to travel logs, although she mostly enjoys the escapism of fiction. Her particular joy, is penning descriptive passages. This is her first publication but she hopes not her last!

BV - #0010 - 240621 - C0 - 216/138/12 - PB - 9781913425791 - Matt Lamination